dragon palace

dragon palace

Hiromi Kawakami

translated by Ted Goossen

Stone Bridge Press • Berkeley, California

Published by
Stone Bridge Press
P. O. Box 8208, Berkeley, CA 94707
TEL 510-524-8732 • sbp@stonebridge.com • www.stonebridge.com

The MONKEY imprint was established by Stone Bridge Press in partnership with MONKEY New Writing from Japan.

Cover design by Counterpunch Inc. / Nick Vitacco (www.counterpunch.ca). Octopus photo by Jade Flesher, via Pexels.

"Dragon Palace" was first published in volume 3 of *Monkey Business* (2013). "Sea Horse" was first published in volume 2 of *MONKEY New Writing from Japan* (2021).

Originally published in Japan as *Ryugu*. Original Japanese text ©2002 Hiromi Kawakami.

English translation © 2023 Ted Goossen.

First printing 2023.

Printed in the United States of America.

p-ISBN 978-1-7376253-5-3 (paperback)
p-ISBN 978-1-7376253-7-7 (casebound)
e-ISBN: 978-1-7376253-6-0 (ebook)

Hokusai

IF YOU turn where the guardrail breaks off and walk down the stone steps from the highway, you'll come upon a rotting fishing boat lying on its side in the sand. On windy days, you can hear its net flapping. I call it a net, but it's a net in name only, for it's full of holes and beginning to unravel. Like the boat, it has been cast away, abandoned.

It has become my habit to walk down those steps to the beach on days when the wind whips up. The waves are rougher then, and higher. The orange trees planted along the highway sway in the gusts. When laden with fruit, their branches bow even more deeply, moving as one.

No one is on the beach. Tangled balls of fishing line and stray clumps of washed-up kelp, tossed to and fro by the gale, scrape across the sand.

Waves flash white as they crash against the rocks on the shore. I try to look at each wave as separate and distinct, but there comes a moment when they merge—each resembles the one that came before, while the one that follows is no different. When this happens, time grinds to a halt, and I feel as though I am reliving the same moment over and over again. If it's six o'clock, for example, I can mentally board the wave that rolls in at that precise moment, travel the short distance from its belly to the crest, then repeat that movement with each six o'clock wave that comes after.

"Hey, buddy!" It was shortly after noon on one of those stormy days when the man called out to me.

The wind was fierce, with a bit of rain mixed in. Not a soul should have been there. How could he have materialized out of nowhere?

"Why so serious?" he asked.

I had fallen under the spell of the rough sea, enfolded in the kind of frozen moment I have just described.

The man was peering up into my face. He was half a head shorter than me, with hair about an inch long. Wet from the rain, it gleamed in the dull light. I guessed him to be about fifty years old.

"Stand that close and the sea'll sweep you away."

He was in my face, so I took a step back toward the water. He moved in again. I retreated further, but he followed me. I took a third step back and, for a third time, he crowded me.

"Hey, watch out. You're askin' for trouble, gettin' so near the waves!"

You're the one pushing me into the water, I wanted to say. But my tongue was like wood in my mouth.

My problem talking had grown more acute the previous year, when I had given up my company job and moved back home. My first job had lasted seven years. My next lasted less than a year. I had grown restless in a mere six months, after which there was no way to continue. Once I had quit that last job, though, I couldn't find another, in part because the economy had gone downhill. Neither my father nor my mother lectured or criticized me, yet their grief at my present situation filled our home. I became more and more tongue-tied.

"You got any money on you?" the man asked.

"A little," I managed to get out.

"You can stand me for drinks, then," he said, thrusting his

clipped head up toward my nose. It looked like we were going to collide.

"Stand you?" I repeated. I studied his face for the first time.

Compared to the forceful impression left by his crewcut, his features somehow lacked focus. His mouth and his nose were too far apart. His eyebrows drooped at the corners. The slackness of his mouth left him with a perpetual smirk.

"You'll have to stand me for the drinks. I'm flat broke," he said, grabbing my arm. I was going to shake him off—he didn't look strong—but then I changed my mind and decided to go with him.

The man headed up the stone steps to the highway. Trucks and motorbikes were roaring past. He and I stood there patiently, waiting for a gap in the traffic.

ALTHOUGH IT was still early afternoon, a red lantern hung from the eaves of the bar at the end of the alley, indicating it was open. The bar's name was written on the lantern in hiragana: Minami. Usually, that means "south," but the fishing tackle shop next door had the same name written with the characters for "beautiful" and "ordinary." I guessed the two businesses were run by the same owner.

The man flung open the door. Inside was dimly lit, and the figure of a beckoning cat perched on the counter. An oddly large beckoning cat. Two other customers sat facing each other on the raised tatami platform. Beside them was a cooler and fishing rods in carrying cases. It seemed the wind was too strong for boats to go out that day, so there wasn't much for them to do.

"Shochu," the man said to the older woman behind the counter. "How about you, buddy," he asked, turning to me. "Same for you?" When I nodded, he craned his neck back across the counter and said, "Make that two." Then, in a low voice, to me again, "How much are you carryin'?"

I checked my wallet. I had a few bills in my back pocket, but I wasn't about to let him know about those. The coins in my wallet added up to 1,750 yen, with another 13 yen in small change.

"I'll look after the bill," he said, quickly extracting the larger coins while casting a sidelong glance at the 13 yen. He jangled the money in his palm.

"Two glasses of shochu comes to 460 yen," he said, counting out the money and placing it on the counter. The woman swept it up with a practiced hand.

"They don't trust me here," he said. We sipped our drinks, shochu cut with hot water. The woman behind the counter was smiling.

"Is it true?" I asked. "You don't trust him?"

"Not for a moment," she shot back.

We drank there for an hour while nibbling on *shiokara*, fermented and salted squid innards. After our third glass of shochu, only 20 yen remained in the man's palm. The disappointed fishermen were long gone, while at some point the woman had retreated to the back of the shop. The man hadn't drunk all that much, but his face was scarlet. He sat there clutching the 20 yen in his left hand and his glass in his right.

"Want to hear a cool story?" he said all of a sudden.

"A cool story?" I asked. He nodded. He had turned into a squishy, blurry thing that undulated before my eyes.

Was I drunk? His whole body was acting bizarre—his arms stretched and shrank, while the top of his head went from round to square, then back to round again.

"First, you've gotta sit down," said the shape-shifting man. I'm already sitting, I protested. He cleared his throat.

"Now listen carefully, and don't talk back," he said, adopting a schoolteacher's tone. I stood up and then sat down again. He cleared his throat one more time. Then he launched into his cool story.

"I WAS an octopus back then," he began. "So, my story could be called an octopus's great adventure.

"At the time I was living on the ocean floor. Small fish made their home there as well, and shrimp and baby crabs, so I had everything I needed. Every so often, humans would lower an octopus pot down to where we were and one of my unluckier comrades would crawl in, but I never fell for that cheap trick. You know what makes a good octopus pot?"

"No," I said. The man cleared his throat again.

"It has to be spotless, no sea anemones or brown algae or anything like that."

Cleanliness was key, the man said. I did my best to look impressed.

"Anyone would be tempted when something so big and shiny and sweet-smellin' comes floatin' down from the surface, even yours truly. I fought off the temptation time and time again, but one day I finally crawled in. That was my big mistake."

The man glared at me. I didn't see why I deserved to be glared at, but there wasn't a whole lot I could do about it.

"They pulled the trap up, and were about to rip me out

and bash me over the head. But at the last moment, I managed to stick one leg out and grab hold of the side of the boat. I slithered out of the pot and used my suckers to cling to the boat's bottom. The humans tried everything they could think of to make me let go—yanked my legs and my head, pelted me with curses—but they were no match for my suckers, so in the end they gave up. Patience and focus—those are the only things that really count."

I was being lectured to by an octopus! Nevertheless, I meekly nodded.

"I held on like that all the way to port, and after they moored the boat. Then at night I slipped away. An octopus is a lot quicker than you might think. I'd heard that sweet potatoes were great eating, so I headed straight for a sweet potato patch."

"Were they really that good?" I asked. "Did they give you strength?"

"Their flesh was hard. But they filled my belly. I didn't care if they were nutritious or not. There was a woman there in the field who I found strangely seductive. So, I went and wrapped myself around her."

"Wrapped yourself around her," I parroted.

"Yeah, and she really got into it. Seducin' a woman is child's play, really. As long as you have the legs for it, that is. Now I've got only two, so it's a tad more difficult. Even so, I know what I'm doing—when it comes to women, prithee leave it to me."

Prithee? Give me a break! Yet come to think of it, there was something octopus-like about the man's face. And the way his soft, malleable body was constantly changing shape made me feel that, yes, he just might be the real deal. As he talked, the tips of his arms and legs changed, sprouting small suckers and turning transparent—now they truly resembled the legs of an octopus.

"Have you seen that picture of the octopus twining itself around a naked pearl diver? That was me. It was made by Katsushika somebody. Know what I'm talking about?"

"Yes, I'm familiar with Hokusai's print," I answered.

He beamed with pride. "That's great—I can see you're an educated man. But let's give the story a rest for now. I can always pick it up again later. Bear that in mind!"

The wind had become even more fierce. The short curtain hanging at the entrance of the bar was flapping madly. Almost no shochu remained in our glasses. The man was clutching the two 10-yen coins that remained. When he relaxed his grip, I could see them glittering in his sweaty palms.

"Hey, buddy, don'tcha have any more money?" he asked. Now that the octopus story was over, he was back to his old way of speaking. When I answered yes, I have a little, his body got all soft and blurry again. "Then let's move on. Still your treat," he said.

We left Minami and went on to the next establishment.

THAT TURNED out to be an izakaya near the train station. It was some distance away. The man staggered on ahead. I followed, wondering how on earth I could ditch him.

The man and I were the first customers of the day. The place could seat about fifty people. One of the waiters tried to show us to a table for two, but the man headed straight for the counter.

"'Tis important to see the chef at his craft," he said. The man's manner of speaking seemed to be in constant flux. And what was this about the "chef" and his "craft"? This drinking spot was part of a chain that had branches all over. What could possibly be worth watching?

The man started ordering. *Shiokara* and dried squid. Squid with fermented soybeans and grilled squid livers.

"It's all squid, isn't it?" I said.

"You got the picture."

"Is it connected to the fact that you used to be an octopus?"

"I guess you could say that."

The man appeared intent on spending my money. At the place before, we had paid after each round, but now he was ordering dishes one after another.

"Hey, buddy," he said all of a sudden, "how come you're so moody?"

"Me, moody? Th-that's not true," I stammered. It irritated me to be pigeonholed by someone like him. Yet in truth I was prone to tumbling into a dark sinkhole of depression. No one could help me then, which helped explain why I was having such trouble talking. Instead, I headed out to wherever I could be alone, like the beach on stormy days.

"I'll be your guide," he said, foam clinging to the corners of his mouth.

"I don't need a guide," I said sullenly, swallowing another mouthful of beer. I thought of getting up to leave then and there, but he leaned toward me, his shape shifting once again, and I lost that chance.

"No need to be polite. I'm happy to do it," he said, jumping up from his counter seat. All the plates of the food we had eaten—the *shiokara* and dried squid, the squid with fermented soybeans and grilled squid livers—looked as though they had been wiped clean.

"Did you lick them?" I asked.

"Naw, no need for that," he said shaking his head. "I wiped them with my tentacles is all."

"But you're not an octopus now."

"Sometimes I revert. My body still isn't at home in the human world," he explained as he slipped past the cashier and hurried out the door. I scrambled to pay our tab. The staff had witnessed him flee, and now they were looking at me suspiciously, which ticked me off.

He was standing outside the izakaya, cool as a cucumber. "You say you're still not used to our world," I pestered him. "So how long have you been a human?"

"Two hundred years, give or take."

"Isn't that more than enough time to adjust?"

"One year for an octopus is a hundred years for a human being."

"Oh, come on."

No sooner had I said that than the man's appearance changed. His red face got redder and redder until it was tinged with black; then the black came to predominate. It was as if I had provoked the wrath of Fudo, the fearsome warrior god.

"Sit down there," the man roared. Where, on the ground? There's no place to sit, I grumbled. That only made him angrier. What could I do? A kids' playground was next door to the izakaya, so I went there and climbed on top of a concrete squirrel. It was slippery and terribly hard to sit on, but there were no other options.

The man followed me. Then, for a second time, he launched into the story of his life as an octopus.

"MY ADVENTURES continued. We octopi are equipped to handle a life full of ups and downs. And we are wrapped in mystery, a universal presence. A creature of myth, you could even say."

Whether I could say that or not seemed quite beside the point, I thought, as I glumly straddled the squirrel's slippery back.

"When I discovered how easy it was to satisfy a woman, I decided to become a man. I had already developed a taste for sweet potatoes, but now I wanted to head down to the river's edge to try what they called sushi. My woman brought me some clothes, and I put them on. They were tattered and torn, but I still looked good in them. It was at that point I became human. Bear that in mind!"

The man aimed a kick at the tail of my squirrel. He was fuming.

"I moved into the woman's tenement with her, ate the sushi, tried soba noodles. Steamed sweet potatoes are delicious too. You've gotta remember to steam them, though. Got it?"

"Yeah, I've got it," I said grudgingly. If I didn't agree, he might turn his fury on me. The last thing I wanted was to end up wrestling and kicking on the ground.

"The woman started givin' me the cold shoulder just because I said I was an octopus. She hooked up with a new lover. Me not makin' any money was a problem too. Anyway, she tossed me out of her place and brought in the new guy.

The other residents of the tenement came to gawk at the man who'd been cast out in nothing but his loincloth. I wept. I hadn't shed a tear in all my years as an octopus, and yet . . . Humans are a species that spend their lives in tears. Like you, for example. Bear that in mind!"

His lecture was putting me in a foul mood. It felt as if my own failings had been laid bare and set alongside those of an octopus. I wanted to escape this loser as soon as possible and head back to the solitude of my windswept beach. I really did.

"After the woman threw me out, I went back to my octopus form and hid out in the estuary, where I could get by eatin' small fish. In the evenings, though, I took human form to clamber up on shore and raid the sweet potato fields. Humans can't handle them raw, though, so I would have to turn back into an octopus there in the field to eat them. One time, a streetwalker bumped into me there. She screamed bloody murder, so I beat a hasty retreat back to the river. I thought I was done with women, but it didn't take long for my desire to return. I became a human again and lived on dry land. This time, though, I had to find a way to make money. I studied my options. I spotted a good-looking woman, followed her home and slipped into her room. She was delighted. And since this time I was pulling in some dough, she didn't kick me out in my loincloth like the first one did either. My business was findin' bell crickets with good voices, training 'em and then hawking 'em on the street. Octopi are good at raisin' insects. We can raise dogs too. And cows and horses. Cats, though, are another thing. We can't deal with those. There are hardly any here, so I can rest easy. When I was livin' in Owari, though, the beach was crawlin' with cats. I had no idea how to handle them."

The man stopped for a moment, lost in thought. He may well have been recalling the cats of Owari.

"I did well with the crickets. Success followed success, and I became rich. Then the woman ran off with my money. Took my luck with her as well. One of my competitors invented a new diet that made his crickets' voices even better. I lost all my customers. Without a woman to look after things, my house became a total mess. Stray cats wandered in and out. Thieves too. A beggar I had never seen before moved in, but I was too depressed to care. I cried to myself from morning till night, rememberin' my days as an octopus. It got so bad that the beggar took it upon himself to lecture me about how to fix my life. Finally, I made up my mind—I would return to the sea.

"This is all of the octopus's adventures that I can share with you now. There may well be other opportunities, though. Bear that in mind!"

The man delivered these last lines while standing stiffly at attention. I sighed. He ignored me. Hey, buddy, let's go check out another place, he said, and went striding away. I sat there on the squirrel for a moment, then gave up and trotted after him. I still had a little money, just enough, I figured, to cover the bill at our next stop. Once that was gone, then I could ditch him. Yet a part of me was beginning to get attached to the guy. Hanging out with someone who claimed to have been an octopus helped provide a distance between myself and the realm of human reason. That way, maybe, I could steer clear of the pollution of this floating world. Such, at least, was the seed of the plan sprouting in my mind.

THE NEXT place the man took me was a grubby Chinese joint. Its name, Kadoya Ichiban, was written in black on the yellow curtain at the entrance.

"I'll have the Squid Curry Ramen," the man said. "Hey, buddy, like some gyoza to go with that?" Before I had a chance to answer, he had already added it to our order. I didn't order anything—I was already stuffed.

Elbows propped on the greasy tabletop, the man drew his face close to mine. "You've got deep lines on your forehead," he said. "What's buggin' you anyway? Instead of frownin' like that, how about we go look for some women to fool around with?"

The Squid Curry Ramen was a ghastly concoction, like Curry Udon except with ramen instead of udon noodles and shreds of what might have been squid floating in the broth.

"How about some squid?" The man thrust a piece of the suspect squid toward me with his chopsticks. I found it impossible to say no.

"Open up," he said, and deposited it in my mouth. I chomped away. "That squid'll give you the strength; then we can go out and find some women to party with."

"But I'm out of money," I said.

"Not a problem," the man replied, sticking his thumb between his middle and index finger in an obscene gesture.

"How can we party without money?"

"Just leave it to me."

The man polished off the dumplings and the Squid Curry Ramen. I paid the bill, which left me with a single thousand-yen note.

"I'm heading home," I said. It was blowing even harder

than earlier in the day. The wooden delivery box on the motorbike parked outside was swinging back and forth in the gathering dusk.

"Hang on there for a minute, buddy," the man said with a serious expression. "Are you tryin' to tell me you don't like women?"

"Women!" I spat out. His adolescent naivete was grating on my nerves. Enough was enough. Why did I have to waste any more time on him? Yet at the same time I found it hard to part ways.

"You've been a prince, so give me a chance to repay you," the man said, inching closer. His body was once again an undulating, shape-shifting blob. Exactly like an octopus. Perhaps he truly was one.

"This way," he said, so I followed him down a narrow jumbled alley that ran behind the station. The smell of fish was everywhere. When we reached the dark end of the alley, he came to a halt. Jerking his chin, he signaled me to stand next to him. I did as he asked. What choice did I have?

The alley must have been a shortcut to the station, given how many people were walking past. For a while, the man just stood there looking at them. When a woman went by, he would stare. He seemed to be muttering something, so I pricked my ears to hear.

"Not that one—twenty points—too stuck-up—first class." When he realized I was listening in, he raised his voice a little. "Soft body—thirty-two points—forty-seven—only so-so." He gave me a wink as if to say, give it a try, buddy—it's by rating them like this that you'll find the one best for you. The man was pushing me to stand in the dark in that godforsaken spot and rate the women who passed. That was either presumptuous or pathetic—I couldn't decide which.

"Sixty-three points," I said after the umpteenth women had walked by.

"That's too high, isn't it?" the man said. "Of course, if she's your type . . ."

I felt strangely liberated. I stood there assigning numbers and adjectives to each woman that came by, one after another. In the process, they stopped being individuals with personalities and real lives. Rather, each woman who strolled past was simply a body and nothing more. But then what was I but one more strolling object: an assortment of features—two eyes, a nose, etcetera—atop a malleable, blob-like body?

The man and I stood there in the dark in our shape-shifting bodies, rating the passing women.

HOW LONG did we go on like that? Two hours maybe? By the end, it was pitch dark. The wind grew. The number of women walking through the alley shrank.

Their faces as they passed beneath the streetlight were no more than a blur. Their clothes were being whipped around by the gale.

"That's the one," the man said. "Let's party with her."

We set off after the woman, who had already turned from the alley onto an even darker back street. She had a big butt.

"She's a woman with a heart, that's for sure," the man whispered to me.

"But how on earth can we get her?" I asked. The man put a finger to his lips to shush me. Then he lengthened his stride until he was walking beside her.

"Hey, baby," he began. She ignored him. Her pace increased.

"Hey, baby. Wanna have a good time?"

She broke into a run. He ran after her. I followed. Two men hot on the tail of a fleeing woman—that was the picture we made. Her back had lost its clear shape, become blob-like. I sensed she was panicking. She seemed to be sweating. There in the dark, I could smell her on the wind.

"C'mon, baby. There's nothin' to be afraid of," the man called. She didn't turn around, just kept running blindly ahead.

We pursued her intently. She fled just as intently. Her silhouette became distinct only when she passed beneath a streetlamp. As those lamps grew fewer and farther between, her form began to blend with the night. At that point, all we had to go by was her scent, yet we didn't abandon our chase.

"C'mon, baby!" the man called again. I thought I heard her gasp. But it could have been the wind, now blowing even more violently. Maybe there was no woman at all. But we ran on in hot pursuit, there in the dark, guided only by the scent of a woman.

We ran and ran until, finally, we arrived back at the beach. We hadn't gone down the steps from the highway but instead had circled all the way around until, suddenly, there we were. The wind howled. The waves roared. Nothing resembling a woman could be seen anywhere. The man and I stood together on the sand, staring at the waves.

"LET ME tell you more of my adventures as an octopus," the man snapped. "Pay close attention!" The waves were now so high, they threatened to sweep us away. I retreated a step, but the man stayed put.

"The octopus never returned to the sea. He'd become completely human. Two years for an octopus is two hundred for a human being. So it wasn't that long, but the change was permanent. I can't remember what life as an octopus was like. I am a man who loves women. Women are soft, cruel, delightfully thoughtless creatures. A man's worth hinges on how much pleasure he can give them. People who dismiss this as old-fashioned don't have a clue. I have my own ideas about things. You best go your own way, buddy. My ocean floor refuge is gone for good, so I'll stick to my ramblin' ways. Bein' human is painful. I wish I could go back to bein' an octopus. But I can't. When water is spilled, it's gone—you can't put it back in the pot. Bear that in mind!"

The wind was raging. You can't put spilled water back in the pot, I repeated after him. On the beach, sea lice swarmed from the rotting boat. The man's body changed shape as the wind battered it. I thought of my father and mother quietly waiting at home for my return.

"It's high time I returned to the octopus world. Women have no more use for me. So, there's no more point in being human. I have my own path to tread. And you have yours. Understood?"

The man seemed to be sinking into the sand as he walked toward me. His body was still in flux. He stuck his hand in my back pocket and extracted the last thousand-yen note. Unfolding it, he held it up in the wind. It fluttered wildly.

"Let's see the 13 yen as well."

He was right—that's exactly how much I had left in my

wallet. No problem with his memory, for sure! I gave him the coins. That left me tapped out.

"Now I will go back to being an octopus. The floating world of humans has been too painful. But there was one thing good about it. Women. You know what makes a woman's octopus pot so special?"

"No," I said. He cleared his throat.

"It's so very clean—no anemones or brown algae down there."

The man was so close that the top of his head almost touched my jaw. His cropped salt-and-pepper hair shone in the night rain. "Waah!" He let out a loud, piercing cry. I was so surprised that I toppled backward in the sand. While I was struggling to my feet, he took off. He did not head toward the ocean, nor veer toward the land. He simply vanished into the night.

I SLOWLY stood up as the ocean gusts buffeted my body. I could still hear the woman gasp. It came to me through the wind. I thought of my father. I thought of my mother. I thought of the women whose lives had touched mine. I thought of the man's words: "Walk your own path!" As I climbed the stone steps to the highway, my own body began to change, becoming soft and squishy. A searchlight spun round and round, illuminating the ocean's surface in an unending circle. As I walked along the highway, my shape continued to undulate. Truck after truck passed me as I trudged along, their loads held down by tarps.

Dragon Palace

GREAT-GRANDMOTHER ITO paid me a visit.

ITO HAD seen the Buddha in a dream at the age of fourteen, after which she began uttering words that came to her from the spirit realm.

> *Weasels and white clouds by night.*
> *Badgers and black clouds by day.*

Ito would wail enigmatic phrases like these several times a day. Her body shook, her eyes stared into space.

Word got around, and people began to worship her. Two particularly devoted followers, a man and a woman, moved into her family's house. They confined her to a storeroom, which they shared with her, on the east side of the house, away from her parents, brothers, and sisters. Then, without consulting anyone, they knocked a hole in the wall so that they could pay reverence to the rising sun each morning.

With the approach of winter, the storeroom grew very cold. Frost covered Ito's quilt and that of the couple as well. To stay warm, the couple made love again and again. Ito had no idea what all the panting and moaning was about.

One night, a hand reached up and caressed Ito's bottom as she was squatting over the chamber pot, peeing. She had been strictly forbidden to step outside the storeroom at night. Doing so, the woman warned her, would reduce her sacred power. It was because she ventured outdoors after sundown that the divine words were coming to her less often. The night air was sapping her spiritual strength—so the woman said.

Cooped up like that, Ito spent almost all her time sleeping. As her sleep was shallow, she used the chamber pot frequently. But peeing made her thirsty, causing her to gulp water from the jug beside her pillow. She would fall back asleep and then wake up to use the chamber pot again. Next to her the man and woman continued their lovemaking.

The hand that caressed Ito's bottom belonged to the woman. Please come and join us, Your Holiness, she said. So Ito wiped herself and hopped into the couple's bed. It was her introduction to sex. Sandwiched between the couple, she couldn't tell where the man ended and the woman began. They copulated all night long.

"GREAT-GRANDMOTHER," I called. Ito opened her eyes.

She had appeared to me in miniature form, so small she barely reached my knee. She had the translucent skin of a fourteen-year-old and black hair that was long and straight. Ito was beautiful. It was not hard to see why worshippers flocked to hear whatever came out of this girl's mouth, whether the words were divine or not.

"You're a common wench, aren't you," Ito spat out, looking me over. "And yet you tell me you're my great-granddaughter."

I laughed, which only irritated her more.

"What does a lowly housewife have to laugh about?" she said with an indignant frown.

Her words were biting, but the fact that she only came up to my knee made them toothless, however harsh she sounded. I knelt and caressed her hair.

Ito responded like a cat whose neck was being stroked, craning in my direction. Her eyes closed and her lips parted.

"My powers came back to me," said my knee-high great-grandmother, resuming her story.

SLEEPING WITH the couple revived Ito's flagging spiritual strength. It suited her physically. And once she had grown used to the three-way sex, she realized it was far less complicated than she had thought at first. You could vary the strength and the angle of the ins and the outs, as it were, position yourself on top or underneath, on the side or diagonally, and that was about it.

As Ito tired of the arrangement, she began to draw away from the couple. Her devotees had increased to the point that her house was packed with them. Frightened by her wails, her family had moved to a distant village. She and they were made of different stuff.

"THEY WERE common through and through, all of them," Ito's voice rose from the vicinity of my knee.

Ito seemed to detest anything common. When I laughed the same laugh I had before, I received a threatening hiss.

ITO USED sex, unlimited amounts of it, to control her followers. She would summon whomever she had chosen and invite them to her bed. Most served her reverentially, but a few declined.

> *The cicada in the ground runs.*
> *The ear of the horse sinks.*

Ito directed mysterious words like these at anyone who tried to resist. All feared their power. No one could refuse that voice. She copulated with every devotee who shared her home, making no distinction between men and women.

On one occasion, a typhoon blew the roof off her house. Rain poured down on her and her followers. Ito went to the storeroom and began spinning like a top, so that her kimono rose above her ankles. She circled the storeroom in this manner. When a devotee asked why Her Holiness was behaving so, she beat him. Yet even as she delivered the blows she never stopped spinning. She spun out the door and down the corridor to the front entrance, where she kicked in the doorframe and smashed the door with a tremendous clatter; then, with blood trickling down her arms and cheeks, she exited through the gate. When she hit the road she was still spinning.

She went on like that, spinning around and around through the storm, until she reached the village on the shore.

"I WANT some fried pork," Ito said out of the blue.

"Some what?"

"Pork. I asked for some pork."

Her request caught me by surprise. It sounded like a new sort of divine incantation, but in fact it appeared she simply wanted to eat pork. I grabbed my purse and headed for the door, intending to pick up a ready-cooked pork cutlet at the store, but Ito stopped me.

"It has to be cooked fresh," she said, pointing straight ahead at the refrigerator.

The nails on her tiny fingertips were a pale pink. She was like a finely crafted toy. Maybe she had a windup key on her back. I touched her there to make sure. But all I felt were shoulder blades—no windup key.

I knew there were cutlets in the meat compartment. Three, stacked one on top of the other. Could Ito see them? I opened the fridge door, pulled out the meat, and cut the tendons to make it tender. When I began stirring the eggs, Ito said she wanted to help.

I put my hands under her arms and picked her up. She weighed no more than a large cat. Ito stirred the yolks and whites with a pair of cooking chopsticks. Squaring her shoulders, she threw herself into the stirring.

When my arms got tired and I set her down, she hissed at me again. Her face was like that of a fox or badger. I was mixed up in something strange indeed.

My relatives often talked about Ito when we gathered for funerals and Buddhist memorial services. It wasn't the usual exchange of news about this and that happening to so-and-so. Rather, it was like the stories told around the hearth in olden times, where a single episode was related from start to finish. Ito was my great-grandmother; in other words, my mother's mother's mother. Not that distant a tie. Yet I couldn't imagine us being connected to each other. Both my mother and her mother were, to use Ito's words, "common housewives."

Ito watched intently as I dredged the pork in breadcrumbs and slid it into the hot oil. "It's sizzling," she murmured, standing on her tiptoes. Even then she was too short to see into the pan. She poked my thigh. What could I do? I picked her up again. She stared with great seriousness at the fine bubbles rising to the surface. When the pork floated up

I scooped it from the oil with a wire net and drained it for a moment. Ito reached out to touch the cooked cutlet.

"Ouch, it's hot!" she cried, yanking her hand away.

"Of course it's hot," I said.

She started bawling. "How was I to know?" she sobbed.

"You really didn't know?"

"I lived knowing nothing and died knowing nothing," she said through her tears. I put her down and ran the oil through a paper filter back into its container. Then I sat down on the kitchen floor myself. I placed Ito on my knee and gave her a big hug, patting her gently on the back. She still wouldn't stop bawling, so I rubbed her tiny back a few more times. It was hot to the touch. She cried on and on, her arms wrapped tightly around my waist.

ITO BECAME a beggar in the village on the shore. She was sick to death of the way her followers clung to her. They called her the Foundress but in fact she had taught them nothing. They had only been drawn to those incomprehensible phrases that tumbled from her without her understanding. She was not responsible.

Ito entered a ramshackle fisherman's hut, wrapped herself in tattered nets, and fell asleep. The next morning, she went down to the wharf and scrounged whatever she could from the leftovers of the day's catch. She would set her eyes on a small fish, pounce on it before the cats, wild dogs, and crows could grab it, then scurry away.

When stormy weather made fishing impossible, Ito ate the seaweed she had gathered, or stole the dried fish that the villagers hung from their eaves. If the storms continued, she made the rounds of their back doors and begged for food. When she showed up, the villagers piled leftovers on a plate and set it on the ground outside. They didn't open their doors for anyone or anything else—not dogs, nor cats, nor beggars other than Ito—yet all opened for her. Ito tap-tapped, the door slid open a crack, and a plate was hurriedly thrust outside. On the bare earth. Then, before Ito had a chance to say thank you, the door closed again. Ito ate the food on the spot. Crouching over the plate, she snatched what was on it with her teeth and tongue like an animal, never using her hands. Not once did she carry the food back to her hut.

No sooner had she finished than, as though they had been standing watch, waiting for the opportunity, white hands darted out to take back the plate. Their owner remained hidden. Only the hands emerged and disappeared again. Every house was the same. Ito wondered at times if there were no people in the village, just those inhuman things. Yet when she went to the harbor, there were sunburned fishermen handling the catch, and women who looked like their wives mending the nets and helping to clean the fish. The same scene one would find in any fishing village.

Ito was at the wharf pilfering fish as usual one day when she began to feel strange. Her stomach had hurt since morning, and her movements were sluggish. She had considered staying in bed, but a storm seemed to be on the way, and she wanted to gather what fish she could before the boats were confined to port. But she was slow, and things weren't going as they usually did. Normally, she was quicker than the dogs and crows, but now she moved no faster than the fishermen. That meant she could be detected. By the dogs and crows, and by the people as well. They might catch her and toss her in the sea.

Ito grabbed her fish and fled, but in her haste she ran headlong into one of the fishermen. The impact sent her to the ground where she lay, defenseless, pinned under his foot. She expected him to trample her. Yet he stepped over her without breaking stride as if nothing had happened and continued on to the center of the wharf where the other fishermen were clustered.

The fishermen had not seen her. She was invisible to their eyes. As a test, she walked over to the wooden crate that held the biggest fish and picked one up. No one challenged her. She walked back and forth in front of a group of fishermen who were squatting beside the crate, smoking, but they didn't notice her either, however much she hopped about. Instead, they kept their eyes fixed on other things, like the fish and the women. Her form was undetectable to each and every person there at the wharf.

> *Timbered forests span the stars.*
> *The heavens brim with rain.*

Enigmatic words spewed from Ito's mouth for the first time in months. At that precise moment, the people on the wharf shrank back and looked up toward the sky. Is a great rain coming? several said at once. Is a typhoon on the way? Ito grabbed three big fish and strolled back to her hut. Then she wrapped herself in netting, closed her eyes, and fell fast asleep.

The rain and wind began almost immediately. The villagers were unanimous—the anger of the goddess had brought this about. A family must have failed to give her food when she came to their back door. That, they all agreed, explained her fury.

Ito slept on, oblivious to the world, as beside her the three fish began to rot. When they putrefied, swarms of insects stripped their flesh until only skeletons remained. It was then that Ito finally awoke.

She made the rounds of the villagers' back doors, but there was no one to beg from. While she was sleeping, they had deserted the village.

"CUTLETS ARE delicious, aren't they?" Ito said as she dug into the plate of pork I had cut up for her. I watched as the tiny pieces disappeared between her lips. They were a bright red, although she wore no lipstick.

She polished off the first cutlet in no time, then gobbled up the second. I wasn't sure she could manage the third, but that turned out to be no problem at all.

"Living by the sea, we had only fish to eat. Sentaro used to go on and on about how much he wanted pork."

Who was Sentaro? I doubted Ito would tell me. I dragged the depths of my memory until, at last, I came up with that name's owner.

Sentaro had been Ito's husband. Not long after they began living together, though, Sentaro had suddenly passed away. He had fathered no children with her. Yet Ito had given birth to a number. All were girls, whose fathers were unknown.

"Your grandmother was my third," Ito said, prodding the cabbage with her chopsticks. Cabbage didn't seem to rate among her favorite foods. She was just poking the pile apart. The rice cooker beeped, signaling the rice was ready. Ito threw her arms over her head in alarm. It's just the rice, I said, whereupon she lowered her arms and broke out in a big smile. She sat there so prim and proper, and when she smiled like that she was as cute as could be. Angelic, even.

"Pigheaded she was, that child," Ito said, her smile gone. Now you couldn't tell her age—she could have been fourteen years old, or a hundred.

"That child?"

"Your grandmother."

Now she definitely looked a hundred. Like a mechanical doll, she pushed her cabbage around her plate and peered up at my face. I know who you are, her look said. I know everything about you.

I gave Ito a bowl of rice. She sniffed it, inhaling its aroma.

"It smells funky, doesn't it."

"Funky?"

"But I like it that way," she said, wolfing it down. There could be no doubt—I was mixed up in something strange indeed. Ito asked for one bowl after another. She sprinkled salt on the gleaming rice before shoveling it in her mouth.

ITO BID farewell to the now uninhabited seaside village. The night before she left she gave birth to her first child. Perhaps that explained why her belly had been causing her such problems. The whole time she had been sleeping in the fisherman's hut, it seemed, the baby had been growing inside her belly. Apparently, that had been long enough for it to reach full term.

It was an easy birth. But the baby opened Ito's eyes to how far removed she was from not only her family but from everyone else in the world. The child could walk the moment it was born, and it sang. The songs bore a close resemblance to the incomprehensible words that flowed from Ito's mouth—the difference was its words were set to a tune:

> *The child sprouts at the root.*
> *The peony sprouts at the root.*

Ito found the child creepy. As someone universally regarded as creepy herself, she pitied a child seen like that even by its own mother. Yet her distaste outweighed her pity. She ran away, hoping to leave the child behind. But the child followed. When Ito quickened her steps, the child quickened hers too. Although she had just learned to walk, the child refused to be outpaced, however fast Ito went.

They continued in this manner all the way to the next village. They made the rounds of the villagers' back doors, begging. A door would open a crack and a plate of leftovers would be thrust out. Ito would voraciously devour the entire lot. To prevent her child from cutting in, she huddled over the plate, protecting it with her whole body. The child sang sadly:

> *The child sprouts at the root.*
> *The peony sprouts at the root.*

As if enticed by the song, one of the doors opened a crack and a voice responded: "Oto-sama. Oto-sama. Please quell your anger."

Ito raised her face from the plate of food and shouted: "I'm the damned goddess here! Not this kid."

The child sang even louder.

"Oto-sama. Oto-sama. We implore you. Please, please quell your anger." Grains of uncooked rice came flying from the back door. Ito fell to the ground to retrieve them. She scrambled about to ensure the child would not get a single grain.

The child continued her song.

"Oto-sama. Oto-sama." The voice from inside grew louder. Still singing, the child made a dash for the crack in the door. As she slid toward the opening, a white hand darted out and grabbed the plate that Ito had snatched; then, a split second before the door closed, both child and plate were whisked inside.

The child never returned. The family who took her in prospered for generations thereafter. They built a shrine to her in their home and worshipped her as a god. Every day, they placed brown rice and a fresh fish on the shrine as an offering. Then the family chanted, "Goddess. Sacred Daughter. Goddess," in unison.

The child was gone but Ito's life continued on as before, an endless round of begging. Each back door opened to her now, and a plate piled with more food than she could eat was placed outside. Some houses offered her more than leftovers—piping hot rice, for example, or raw meat. At a certain point she grew bored and left the village. She was pregnant for a second time, possibly because she had taken to waltzing in the front doors of people's homes and sleeping with whoever happened to be there, men and women alike. Ignoring the discomfort in her belly, she chose a steep mountain path as the route for her departure. It was while laboring up that path that the baby came.

"I KNOW all about you," she spat out, waving a palm the size of a Japanese maple leaf in front of my nose.

"About me?"

"I know where you've been, where you're headed, your past and your future."

So Ito claimed to know everything, not just my past—that was bad enough—but my future as well. This strange little being who barely reached my knee could see my whole life, at least according to her.

"All right, let's hear it then," I said, rising to my full height. My shadow loomed over her. In response, Ito reverted to her fourteen-year-old face. The translucent skin, the red lips, the long, glossy hair, the unclouded expression.

"Having been born, you eat, learn, mate, forget, sleep, die," she said in a single breath.

"So what? That's all perfectly ordinary."

"What else could it be but ordinary? You're a common woman, after all."

"Then you shouldn't make such a big deal about it."

"But I never learned anything."

I lived knowing nothing and died knowing nothing, Ito whispered. Because I knew nothing, I forgot nothing. I lived without forgetting and died without forgetting. She whispered and whispered.

I was mixed up in something very strange. It made no sense at all. Ito began sobbing as she had before. Her face like that of an angel. She sobbed and sobbed, and her tears made me pity her. I picked her up and hugged her, wiped her tears, held her between my thighs to warm her. Ito's tiny body was freezing cold. She kept sobbing, her eyes swollen.

SHE GAVE birth to one child after another.

Ito moored the children to her with cords so that none would be pulled into the back doors they visited. She wrapped one end of the cord around each child's waist, the other end around her own. The children grew rapidly. They surpassed her in height in only two or three years; then not long afterward, each child untied herself and moved far away.

Only her third daughter, my grandmother, stayed. She grew slowly, so that three years after her birth she was still only half Ito's height.

> *Let me stand in a garden of red flowers.*
> *Let me stand in a garden of blue flowers.*

Back doors opened wide when her third daughter sang this song. On occasion someone even poked a face out to take a peek. Others would call out to them to take care, bad weather was on the way. One time they were actually invited inside. The person who invited them in was a stout middle-aged woman. She stripped off their tattered clothes in a corner of her kitchen and washed their bodies clean with a basin of hot water. Then she pulled out a set of clean clothes and bade her guests put them on.

This was the first time in a kitchen in a long while for Ito, who had been on the road for ages. She loved it there. Her daughter felt right at home as well. It was so warm and steamy, and it smelled so good.

Ito pounced on the stout woman and strangled her. The woman offered almost no resistance. Then mother and daughter each grabbed a leg, dragged the body to the ocean, tossed it in, and returned, their faces the picture of innocence. There was a fierce storm that night, but the two of them stayed on at the house, ignoring the rough and raging seas.

The next morning the waters were perfectly calm, as if nothing had happened the preceding night. Ito adopted the woman's identity and lived in her home for a number of years.

"MURDERER!" I cried. I peeled Ito from my body and hurled her to the floor. She did not resist. She lay there on the floor like a doll.

I was mixed up in something terribly strange. I wished she would go away. Ito stared at me with eyes like marbles. I stared right back, but her face was impassive.

"It's hardly worth making a fuss about."

"I'll make a fuss, all right."

"It may not have really happened, after all."

True enough. For one thing, her very presence was out of the ordinary. Yet here she was. Whether the things she described had actually taken place or not, I had no desire to have someone who could think of strangling somebody near me, no desire at all.

"Leave!" I demanded.

She gave a contemptuous sniff.

"Disappear!"

"Stop pestering me."

"I'm serious. I want you gone."

"You're a fine one to talk. My blood runs in your veins."

I could feel my heart jump. Something was coming back to me, a memory. But it was lost in fog.

"It's just like you to forget your own deeds," she said. Her voice was cold.

"Forget, you say?"

"What you did, what you didn't do, it's all the same."

"The same?"

"Thinking about doing something is no different than doing it."

"You're wrong."

Yet even as I said this, memories of horrible deeds I had contemplated assailed me. But I hadn't carried them out. Or had I? I was suddenly very worried. I had become mixed up in something very strange. And that strange something was now peering into my inner being. Ito's beautiful, innocent eyes had fixed me in their sights.

THE HOUSE Ito and her third daughter had taken over prospered, so that people in the area came to call it "the palace." The man Ito was living with died, and the daughter married and moved out. As Ito grew old, she forgot more and more of her own past. She would grab whoever happened to be nearby and ask, "Where is it I'm from again?"

"Are you all right, Oto-san?" the person would ask. "You mustn't forget who you are."

"Oto-san, you say? Is that my name?" Everyone would nod in assent.

"You are the Goddess who lives in the palace, the Goddess who is forever young," they chimed in chorus.

Ito took to prowling outside the palace. Her face was smooth, her cheeks lightly rouged, and she smiled as she accosted passersby and pressed them to sleep with her. "Let's do it," she would say brightly, whether they were men or women.

The rumor spread. The goddess of the palace had gone

crazy. Now when she cooed "Let's do it," people looked on her with pity. They gently pushed her arms away when she tried to embrace them. Yet none of them shunned her.

Ito's prowling had taken on a new urgency when a drifter named Kii moved into the gatekeeper's cottage at the palace. No one knew where he was from. The palace had once boasted an extensive staff—gatekeeper, cook, gardener, maids—but with Ito's mental decline first one then another had drifted away, until now no one was left. Nobody objected when Kii took over the cottage.

Ito wasted no time propositioning Kii once she discovered he had moved in. When she said, "Let's do it," his answer was yes. They spent the whole night engaged in sexual intercourse.

Ito and Kii's relationship continued for a year. They made love under the gatekeeper's quilts every night, every evening. Then, a year to the day after their first meeting, Ito woke up at daybreak and looked at the man sleeping beside her.

I've been here too long, she thought. It's time to move on.

Wrapping a thin kimono around her body, Ito headed out the door of the gatekeeper's cottage in her bare feet. She began walking east, toward the rising sun, never once looking back.

ITO BURST out with:

> Weasels and white clouds by night.
> Badgers and black clouds by day.

I covered my ears in alarm.

My leg tickled. When I looked down, I saw Ito had

wrapped her arms and legs around it and was shimmying up. She climbed quickly, chanting her nonsensical words as she went. Now she had reached my waist. When she reached my chest, she peeled back my blouse and began sucking at my nipples.

I was mixed up in something strange indeed.

"Great-grandmother," I said. "You're not really here, are you?"

Ito shook her head. "No, I'm not."

"So then why are you here?"

"You called me, didn't you?" she quietly answered my question with a question of her own.

"I did?" I replied. My voice was equally quiet.

You did.

But then, why?

Don't ask me. I lived knowing nothing and died knowing nothing.

Poor thing.

No sooner had I said this than Ito began to sob.

I was mixed up in something very strange. Now that strange thing was sucking on my breasts with all her might, like a baby. Suckling as she sobbed. Out of pity, I let the strange thing suck away. Out of love, I let her. With Ito still clinging to my breast, I turned eastward and began to walk.

Fox's Den

SHOTA IKEMORI loves *abura-age*, the deep-fried tofu used to make *inari-zushi*, named after the fox deity Inari, since foxes are said to favor this type of sushi. Shota yowls from time to time, his face is long and pointy, and sometimes a white mist billows from his mouth into the air.

I'd feel more comfortable calling him Shota-san instead of Shota, since we're not related or anything, but every time I tell him that, he just shakes his head. So Shota it is.

Since last year, I have been visiting Shota's home as a part-time caregiver. Shota is ninety-three and lives alone. His only close relative is his niece Tatsuko, who is seventy-seven years old herself. The year before last, Tatsuko fell and broke her right leg, after which she supposedly became a little senile. Every so often, Tatsuko will phone Shota and spend over an hour spouting a steady stream of invective about the ways she was mistreated by his older sister—her own mother—dead now for twenty years.

Shota loves to mimic the way she speaks. Mom never should have done what she did; don't do this, she said, don't do that; she was after me all the time; that's why I ended up like this; what's my condition called? That's right, "adult child syndrome," that's what she gave me; I caught it from her; that's why I could never marry.

Adult child syndrome? Shota laughs. What does she mean, she caught it from my sister? It's not a cold, after all! Shota goes on merrily like that, adding his own comments from time to time. Listening to him, I find it hard to believe that Tatsuko is really senile. Rather, it seems she just can't stop talking.

Shota's house has three eight-mat rooms, two six-mat rooms, and a kitchen with an adjoining storeroom, more than big enough for someone living alone, one would think, were it not for the books and magazines piled everywhere. No space is left empty. Books are even stacked under the kitchen sink. Until my arrival, porno magazines and paperbacks filled the bathtub, and Shota used the public bath.

I was able to get him to let me clean out the bathtub, but that was it. "It's a waste to shell out 400 yen every time you bathe," I chided, but he wouldn't budge. It's just once or twice a week, he said, so it doesn't amount to that much. When it comes to money, Shota isn't hard up. He once ran a used bookstore, and keeps a hand in the game by selling books by mail order. He owns other properties too, which he rents out.

"Isn't it sacrilegious to keep books in a bathtub?" I asked him. He laughed at me. Sacrilegious, hell, he said. They're just skin rags.

"But what about the paperbacks?" I said. Shota took a moment to think; then he let out a yowl, that whining, growling bark he uses when someone pushes him to do something.

I work at Shota's two days a week.

SHOTA TAKES daily walks. There is no set route. He simply heads off in a random direction for however long he chooses.

"It's good for your health," I said. Shota's face darkened. You sound like a goddamn NHK announcer, he snorted.

"Could that be Shota-san's secret to a long life?" I went on, ignoring him. Don't call me Shota-san, he fumed.

"Shota's secret to a long life," I corrected myself. Shota nodded at first, but then he turned sullen again.

What would you say to a short-lived person, he asked. The secret to your short life?

"If you put it that way, no."

What you can't say to men, you can't say to women, Shota told me. What you can't say to the short-lived, you can't say to the long-lived either. The vacuum cleaner drowned out my lukewarm response. Shota stalked off to his six-mat room in a huff. The northernmost of the two six-mat rooms was where his futon was permanently laid out, with ten ashtrays at its head. Shota smoked his cigarettes down to the butt. They were lights, very low in tar. When he finished one, he would jam it down hard to put it out, so that each filter formed a right angle in the ashtray. Cleaning the ashtrays was part of my job. All ten were always full to the brim.

I sometimes accompany Shota on his walks. He asks me along. You've done enough cleaning, he says. Today, you can keep me company.

Shota puts on his cap and a cardigan sweater. Then he grabs his cane and takes off. He walks at a rapid pace, despite the cane. And he wants to hold my hand.

"No way!" I say, whereupon his tone changes. How can you deny an old man, he wheedles, his voice pitiful. I'm begging you.

What can I do? I extend my hand, and he grabs it immediately. His hand is dry, and big. He is a big man.

"My, what big hands you have," I say. He nods. "Not an old man's hands at all."

He frowns. Cut that old man crap.

"But you were just playing the 'poor old man' game."

I use whatever works, he says.

We come to a house whose gate is encircled with roses. They're beautiful, aren't they? he says.

"Yes, they are."

Smell good too.

"They certainly do."

I wanted to show them to you.

"Thank you."

How many times a year do you have sex?

"What?"

I slap his hand away. Shota just stands there. A white mist rises from his mouth. It looks like white smoke. It's not cigarette smoke, though. Shota never smokes on his walks. He only smokes in bed.

Shota yowls.

"You've crossed the line," I say. "You can't ask a caregiver such things." He gives a distracted nod. His mind is elsewhere; the words had just drifted out of his mouth. Sorry, just go on home ahead of me, he mumbles.

I hurry back and rush through the rest of my cleaning. I work for a number of people, and surprisingly, more than a few act like Shota. Not everyone, and not only old people—you find such behavior among the young as well. When it comes to humans, I guess it takes all kinds.

I waited a while, but Shota didn't come back. So I draped a cloth over his dinner and left a note telling him to heat up the soup. Shota's house smells of mildew. The musty odor of old books. How was Shota spending his days when I wasn't around? I tried to imagine, but couldn't. I loved him a bit, I guess. I didn't like his yowling, though.

I'M FIFTY-THREE. Forty years younger than Shota. I'm not a big woman, but I am strong. Working as a caregiver is right up my alley. I'm no good working with other people in any kind of group setting. Sex? A few times a year. Eight times last year, if I remember correctly. My partner is a man I used to work with. I always have to wait for him to get in touch with me, though. I'm never the one contacting him. For one thing, I don't know his phone number. I have no desire to find out, either.

When Shota asked about my sex life, the last thing I wanted to do was mention the eight times.

During the five days a week that I don't see him, I find myself fantasizing about Shota more and more. I regain my composure and my distance, though, when I see him in the flesh.

Would you get mad if I asked to see you naked? Shota questioned me one time. He said this in an almost comically serious tone.

"Aren't you being a little too forward?"

How so?

"Why must you see me naked?"

Because I love you.

"So, if you love a woman the first thing you want is to see her naked?"

Old people like me have no time to waste.

"Aha! Once again, you act old only when it's convenient."

All right, then, let me put it another way. It's because I'm a frank and open sort of guy. I don't dress things up.

I laughed, but I kept vacuuming. Please strip for me, he asked again.

"Okay, when I've finished my cleaning," I replied. It's a deal, then, he said with a grin. Shota's face is pointy and deeply furrowed. He has a beautiful voice, relaxed and resonant.

When I finished cleaning up, I removed my clothes. My body looks good, if I say so myself. It's pure white, and though my tummy sticks out a bit, I'd be quite okay parading my nakedness in front of the world. So why not to Shota?

You're beautiful naked. May I touch you?

"Sure, go ahead." So, he began fondling me. Gently at first, but when I didn't protest, he became more forceful. He certainly knew what he was doing. I became excited, and so did he. But he soon grew tired.

He retired to his six-mat room and his futon. I put my clothes back on and began preparing dinner. What would sleeping with Shota be like? Was it really impossible? I made him the dried daikon with *abura-age* dish that he liked, and added more *abura-age* to the miso soup.

I peeked into his room, but he was fast asleep. Shota sleeps a lot. Like a baby, in fact. Perhaps he spends the days I'm not there sacked out, dead to the world.

THE TURDS of the past, Shota said.

"The turds of the past?"

Yes, they should still be there.

There was an outdoor privy, Shota went on, beside the house in the nearby town where he lived until he went to college. He thought it should still be there. It had been boarded up after a thief had taken refuge in it. The thief hadn't stolen much of value, but the men of the town had him surrounded, so he had no choice but to hole up there overnight. The following morning, he threw a rope over the ceiling beam and hanged himself. Everyone steered clear of the privy after that. Even the nightsoil collectors wouldn't go near the place.

Ever since, the turds of the past have been sitting there, he said. It always scared me.

"Now that you mention it, there were nightsoil collectors back then."

Yes, they carried shit off to fertilize the fields and things like that. Returning it to the soil.

"Now it all gets flushed away."

Flushed and flushed. Sent to meet the water. The sky. The earth.

"You're probably right."

Those turds would have lost their shape, though.

"Ah yes, their shape."

I find it unnerving, Shota went on, to imagine that the turds in the privy beside my old home might have retained their original form.

I was chopping onions as I listened to Shota talk.

"Turds that old may just dry up and turn to dust."

I hadn't thought of that.

"Insects would get at them too."

I hope that's true.

Shota went off to the six-mat room for a cigarette. He sat formally on his futon, legs tucked under him, to smoke. When he had finished the cigarette, he took a sheet of paper and began drawing something on it. After a few minutes, he brought it to the kitchen to show me. It was a sketch of turds. Some were long, some were spiral, some were round. Shota is good at drawing.

There are turds like these in the outdoor privy where I grew up, still.

"You're like a child!" I laughed.

He flushed. I admit the sketches are silly. But am I child-ish in what I say as well? Am I always childish?

"You're not childish at all. You're a fine-looking man," I replied as I peeled the carrots.

I thought a little about the turds of the past. Anything frozen in time provokes anxiety. Ancient turds make me uneasy too. Shota began to yowl. I hurriedly sauteed the carrots and some burdock root. I added broth, mirin, and soy sauce to the pot. I sprinkled chopped green onion over the miso soup. Shota retreated to his room. I could hear him yowling in there, once, twice.

SHOTA'S NIECE Tatsuko was hospitalized.

This time, I was told, the cause was a broken left wrist. That in itself didn't require hospitalization, but she thought she would have trouble looking after herself, so she asked the hospital to admit her.

I was asked to take a change of clothes to her hospital room. Her ground-floor apartment was three stations down the line from Shota's place. It had a small garden. The garden was filled with flowers in full bloom. They lined the short flight of steps leading down from the veranda: purple, pink, white, yellow—you name it. When I looked at them from the window, though, I grew bored in no time flat. I'm not a big fan of cultivated flowers. Perhaps that's connected to my aversion to organized groups: I can't bring myself to like either.

Tatsuko's apartment was clean and tidy. Not a whole lot of books, though. Quite a contrast to Shota's home.

I pulled a set of clean clothes from Tatsuko's chest of

drawers—panties, undershirts, a nightgown, socks—and wrapped them in a *furoshiki* carrying cloth. I had borrowed the cloth from Shota. It was decorated with their family crest. The cloth stank of cigarette smoke. A smoker's belongings are always filled with that odor.

When I entered Tatsuko's hospital room carrying my bundle, I was greeted by an old woman's voice. It came from the occupant of the bed across from Tatsuko's. Why do some people still sound youthful as they age while others don't? Shota's relaxed, resonant voice popped into my head.

Tatsuko was lying there vacantly, her eyes swimming through space. She seemed unable to focus on anything. Her roommate was rattling on and on about someone she couldn't stand. All six beds in the room looked occupied, but the residents of the other four had all closed their curtains. Only Tatsuko and the woman across from her allowed themselves to be seen.

"Good afternoon. It's me, Yasuda," I said. Tatsuko nodded blearily. The old woman in the bed opposite closed her mouth. She was watching us closely.

I placed the underwear, the nightgown, and the rest of the clothing in the small cabinet next to Tatsuko's bed, and the buttercups and asters from her garden in the glass vase I had brought from the desk in her apartment. The other old woman was keeping a close eye on my movements, her mouth hanging open.

I glanced at her, whereupon she rolled on her side. When I looked away again, however, she turned her whole body back to face me, as though on a string. Tatsuko stayed mum throughout.

"Your uncle Shota is well," I said. She managed an almost imperceptible nod.

"Is there anything else that you need?" I asked. Again, no clear response.

The old woman in the bed opposite spoke up. Are you her uncle's wife? she asked me. I smiled and shook my head no. Really? she continued. You never come to see her.

The woman's face was changing into something inhuman. I didn't want to watch, so, still smiling, I bent over and started rubbing Tatsuko's back. I could hear the woman making noises that I couldn't place, but after a while those subsided.

Tatsuko didn't say a word during my visit. Perhaps she had transformed into something that didn't speak. Whatever it was, I was sure it was very soft. Moss, for example, or fresh fallen snow, or a spring breeze.

When I left the room, the face of the other old woman had changed to that of a tiger beetle. I had encountered those beetles on my walks in the hills. Cute little things, for sure, but a tiger beetle's face doesn't suit a human body well at all. I could hear her shrill *gii, gii* again and again as I walked out the door.

SHOTA SEEMED a bit sad when I told him of Tatsuko's condition. So that's the story, he said.

"Still, her complexion is good, and she seems to be in good shape."

Why do we always say old people are "in good shape"? Shota was talking to himself as he looked over a pile of books. "Well written," "witty," "sexy": aren't there other ways to describe these things?

Come to think of it, besides his strolls, Shota spends a lot of time rummaging through his books. When he finally finds what he's looking for, he takes the book back to his room and stretches out on top of his futon to read it. He reads like that for about half an hour. Then I hear him snoring. Shota is well built, a big man. His back is slightly hunched. He sleeps facing the door, with his back to the far end of the room. When I place a cover over his shoulders, he opens his eyes. Ah, he says, and goes back to his book. He is a very focused reader.

"Have you ever been married?" I ask him.

No, I haven't. And you? How about you?

"I married twice, and divorced twice."

And you're only half my age. You've been busy!

"Half your age? A bit more than that, I'd say."

The first of my two husbands was human to the bone— he stank of humanity. He never changed into anything else, no matter what happened. In my heart of hearts, that frightened me. Before long, though, he fell in love with an extremely human (or so he told me) woman like himself and left me. I still remember what a relief it was to have him gone.

Like Shota, my second husband loved *abura-age*. He didn't yowl, but there was something animal-like about the way he moved. I really loved that guy, but, sure enough, he also fell for another woman and flew the coop. It seems I'm just not built to keep a man—they all eventually run away. I see a basic similarity in the natures of Shota and my second ex.

"I've had it with marriage," I said. Shota laughed.

I've had it with almost everything, he murmured. Not just marriage.

"Almost everything? Like what?"

You name it.

Shota made no move to get up. I kept working. A conversation between a recumbent man and a busy woman. For a moment, the world receded from view. I felt like a lonely blade of hoarfrost before the dawn, poised to push its way up through the earth. It left me somehow forlorn, deserted. I wonder if Shota's yowls meant that he felt the same sadness. How about the old woman with the tiger beetle head, and her shrill *gii, gii*?

"Is there anything not included in 'almost everything'?"

Maybe I've still got a few things left to do.

"What sort of things?"

Like seeing you naked.

"You did that the other day, remember?"

Like feeling you up.

"You did that too."

I remember now. I think I really do love you. But what the hell is love, anyway?

"I'm not sure either."

Shota seemed to have shrunk. When my heart turns into a blade of hoarfrost, the world becomes so small. Shota's head looked like the head of an ant, his broad shoulders no wider than a single dandelion petal. Everything felt cold and unfamiliar now. The air, living creatures, objects—everything.

I slipped under Shota's covers. I was so sleepy I couldn't resist. Maybe I caught this sleepiness from him. Side by side, we lay there in the depths of sleep, happily dead to the world.

I QUIT going to Shota's home as a caregiver. Personal relationships between caregivers and clients are forbidden. True, no sex was involved, and there was little chance that we would be discovered, but if someone blabbed about our "personal relationship," I might be fired by my temp agency.

Instead, I began staying over at Shota's two nights a week on an unpaid basis. Shota didn't say yes to this, but he didn't say no, either. In fact, nothing much had changed. The only differences were whether I came during the day or at night, and if I received money or not. I continued to clean the house, prepare dinner, and spend time talking with him. There was no room to lay out another futon, so he allowed me to share his.

When I asked if he would like to see me naked, he usually shook his head no. Sometimes, though, he nodded yes. He seemed fine either way. When the weather was warm, I wore almost nothing. On cold nights, however, I bundled up. It appeared that Shota was no longer able to have sex.

"Don't you feel anything when you see me naked?" I asked him. He grunted.

It feels good, he allowed, but my pecker doesn't answer the call. Maybe my blood flow is the problem. Old age, I bet. I've been around a long time. Everything's weaker, my circulation, my pecker.

Pecker? The word made me laugh. Shota and I fell asleep holding hands. The moment we drifted off, however, our bodies drew apart. We slept back-to-back. We were separate when we slept. We were separate when we were awake. We would be separate when we died. Obviously. Only in those few moments before falling asleep did that distance between us disappear. Then we pressed close together, as if trying to become one body.

I BEGAN leaving for work from Shota's home.

I cleared out of my apartment. I thought of keeping it, but decided it was a waste of money. I knew it would be difficult to find another one at my age. Yet the building would probably be torn down in a few years anyway. At least this way I might be able to stay on in Shota's house after his death. I could claim to be his common-law wife—that should do the trick. I might well die before he did anyway.

Tatsuko left the hospital a little while ago. I suggested that she move in with us (I figured that would help me establish my common-law status), but she politely declined. Instead, she quietly slipped out of the hospital and returned to her apartment. I go there to visit her twice a month. She seems to be in good shape (yep, that's how we compliment old people).

Tatsuko is sure to serve me jasmine tea on my visits. To accompany the tea, she offers me sakura mochi in spring, bean jelly in summer, sugar-coated azuki beans in fall, and steamed buns in winter. Like Shota, Tatsuko is a landlord. Back in the old days, this whole area belonged to the Ikemori family. In fact, it is said that you could walk the entire three-station distance from his house to her apartment without ever stepping on another family's land. That was more than a hundred years ago, however. By Shota's grandparents' generation, the family was already crumbling—the main house splintered and the branch families went their separate ways. Today, only Shota and Tatsuko remain. When they are gone, no more Ikemoris will walk the earth.

I work hard. In all, I cover fifteen homes each week. There is an old person in each. That's because my agency regards senior care as my specialty. There are other people who live in those homes, too. Some are young and some are middle-aged, while others are on the cusp of old age.

Each and every home contains at least one member who has something inhuman about them. Only rarely do I come across a person like my first husband, who is entirely human. It's surprising how many are like Shota. Take the teenage grandson of one of my clients, a tenth-grader, for example. His face is pointy, he loves *abura-age*, and he yowls from time to time.

Tatsuko's lengthy phone calls to Shota came to an end. Or perhaps Shota had been imagining the whole thing, and Tatsuko never phoned him in the first place. Yet this shouldn't be seen as a sign of his advanced age. Heck, I make similar mistakes. So do tenth-graders. We can't remember more than a little of what took place last week. It's said that our recall of childhood events is much clearer, but in fact those memories are hazy too. The flow of time doesn't stop, nor does memory. We do retain some memories from the past, of course, but no one can be sure if they are real or not.

Shota and I are living together. I love him a bit. He says he loves me too. Yet I still can't figure out what love means, what it really is. I do know that I hate his yowling, even now. Our life together would be so much nicer if he'd only cut that out.

EVERY SO often, Shota grabs a few of the porno magazines he used to stash in the bath (they're now heaped in the store-room) and studies them intently.

"Why don't you check out my bod instead," I tease him,

but he just laughs. I laugh too. There's no similarity between my naked body and those of the young women in the magazines—they're completely different things. Shota says it's like the difference between a raw egg and the seal that we use to stamp documents. Both are necessary. Though, he is quick to add, of the two the personal seal is the more important. Shota can display a surprisingly thoughtful side.

The magazines overflow with images of naked young women. Many aren't Japanese. Some are photographed in normal positions, but others are forced to pose in abnormal ways, even beside piles of excrement.

Shota spends the most time engrossed in the ones with excrement. He doesn't spend that much time looking at the girls. He focuses on the shit.

"Are you thinking about the turds of the past?" I ask him. He nods. Since that topic came up, it has often popped into my mind too. That old house in the neighboring town is apparently still standing. No one lives there anymore—it's just a dilapidated shell. Shota is the legal owner of the property. That means, of course, that he owns the privy as well. I've been thinking that you and I could go take a look, he says.

"Take a look?"

Yes, take a look.

Shota's attention is riveted on the excrement in the photographs, and on his earlier sketch of the turds of the past (which he has carefully preserved). Although we still take our daily walks, these days we don't go very far. He is back under the covers within ten minutes, poring over his pictures. All I have to do is look at them, he says, and I'm half asleep. Perhaps it's because they make me feel half dead.

"The poo in the privy is almost eighty years old," I said. "I bet it's evaporated into thin air by now."

No, it wouldn't have evaporated. Could have dried up, though, turned to dust.

Shota seemed obsessed.

"Well then how about if we go take a look this Sunday?" I said. "I could make a box lunch, whip up some *inari-zushi*." Shota was over the moon. A lot happier than when I stripped for him, that's for sure. He yowled a high-pitched yowl. I turned on the vacuum cleaner and pretended not to hear.

THE HOUSE where Shota had lived before entering college turned out to be a real mansion, with dark and gleaming pillars. Back during the heyday of the Ikemori clan, I could imagine people walking back and forth along corridors whose boards creaked as they passed. In the kitchen, the maids would have been cooking rice day and night, the steam rising into the air.

Now, though, the house was a deserted ruin. Spiderwebs hung in every corner, and the smell of mildew was even stronger than in Shota's home. Yet the air inside was bone dry. It appeared that vagrants, thieves, delinquents, and other riff-raff had hung out there, for shoe prints ran along the crumbling halls and across the spongy, decaying tatami mats. How long ago had they been there?

The outdoor privy was tightly sealed. We had brought along tools—a small crowbar and an electric saw—to do the job, but I still couldn't remove a single board. By the time I finally opened a hole big enough to allow us to peer inside, the sun had risen high in the sky.

Exhausted, Shota lay down and fell asleep on the grass. As I watched him lying there, that familiar desolation hit me again, the feeling that I was a lonely blade of hoarfrost poised to break through the surface. Everything seemed so terribly small—Shota, the clouds, the sun. Shota no bigger than a locust, the sun the size of a sesame seed. The locust was sleeping on the grass.

"Shota," I called to him. He didn't respond. "Look, Shota, there's a hole. We can see inside."

But Shota didn't stir. He just lay there on the grass in his tiny locust body. His face was shifting back and forth, now human, now fox. A tiny locust-sized fox face.

The feeling that I had been abandoned was snowballing. Who was there on the grass? Was it really Shota, or just a fox? I peered into the boarded-up privy but couldn't make out much. The shaft of light from the hole I had opened illuminated a spiderweb stretched across the privy's seat. A gnat buzzed nearby.

"No sign of the turds of the past," I called to Shota, but he still didn't budge. Had he died? His face had become that of a fox. Fur seemed to be sprouting from his body, an unpleasant, thick coat, visible in those places not covered by his clothes: the backs of his hands, his neck. Without question, Shota was now a fox pure and simple. Suddenly I was terrified. Terrified by Shota. Terrified by humans in general.

The only way I knew to smoke out a fox spirit was by burning pine needles. I ran to the front of the house to collect them. I gathered up old fallen needles and stripped some young ones off the branches to add to the pile. Then I set a match to the mingled brown and green needles. The fire sputtered to life. The smoke smelled good. The smell that foxes couldn't stand.

Shota stirred. His face was still that of a fox, his body the size of a locust. I felt desolate, forlorn. Frantically, I heaped more needles on the fire. Shota coughed. His eyes snapped open. He yowled. What are you doing? You'll burn the house down.

Shota's body returned to its normal size. His fox face disappeared. I happily tossed more pine needles on the fire. His coughing grew worse. Please, no more needles, he gasped. My terror returned. I knew in that very moment that Tatsuko and Shota were not long for this world. They would die soon. And I would die too, in no time at all. In thirty years, we would all be gone. The old folks I was looking after would be gone too. Heck, even that tenth-grader might be dead by then.

Shota was in pain. The smoke was making him cough. I picked him up (I may be small, but I'm physically strong) and carried him to the front of the house. The smoke wouldn't reach there. Shota was shrinking again. I opened the box lunch and laid out the *inari-zushi* that I had prepared in front of him. I had simmered the *abura-age* skins in sweetened soy sauce. Tiny Shota flew at the sushi. He began munching away. I started munching on them myself.

The ten *inari-zushi* disappeared so fast it was as if we were competing to see who could eat the most. The smoke from the back garden wafted to us on the breeze. Shota dozed off again. I lay down next to him. I wanted to hold his hand, but that doesn't work when the person beside you is the size of a locust. So I picked him up gently and placed him on my palm. We lay there together as if dead. The fire that had started with pine needles was now spreading to the front of the house. Shota yowled. I no longer doubted my love for him. I didn't even mind his yowling. In any case, we all die. We all die. Such were my thoughts as I drowsily watched the flames approach where we lay.

The Kitchen God

I TRIED peeling the kitchen wall with my fingernails, but that didn't work, so I pressed hard with my fingers and a flake of the "stucco," which is what I call it, fell off. I don't know if it's really stucco or not, or even what stucco is precisely, but I like the snappy sound of the word, and that's good enough for me.

I popped the stucco into my mouth. Then I chewed and chewed until, finally, I was able to swallow it.

Once you dislodge the first piece, the rest is easy. Over and over, I stripped flakes of stucco from the crumbling wall and ate them.

"You shouldn't be eating that!" said a voice from under the refrigerator.

That had to be the kitchen god.

A kitchen god is small, has three faces, and lives in the dark corners of the kitchen. The first time I saw one I screamed, which earned me a scolding from my mother. That was before I started first grade. My mother then was younger than I am now.

"You must never be scared of the kitchen god, or neglect him, either," my mother said.

Were kitchen gods common, I wondered. Did they inhabit other people's kitchens, too? My mother never instructed me to keep my mouth shut about ours; nevertheless, I didn't breathe a word about him to Ayaka who lived next door, or to my cousin, Shou.

I'm a grown woman now, but in all these years, I haven't told a soul about the kitchen god. After I got married, I moved into this company apartment with my husband, but it didn't take long for a kitchen god to show up. This kitchen god, however, was unlike the one I had grown up with: the three faces were different, as was the sound of his voice, and its cadence.

"He's here," I told my mother.

"He's present, you mean," she said sternly.

"So, they're everywhere," I said.

"You mean, they are present everywhere."

"It seems they're present everywhere."

"Yes, they are present." My mother lowered her voice. "It's because you have the right attitude, Izumi," she said.

"Attitude?"

"Yes, kitchen gods only inhabit the kitchens of women who display the proper attitude."

My mother hung up with a satisfied click. But was my attitude really so proper? Just that morning, I had stolen a pack of plum chewing gum and an Extra-Large container of miso-flavored Cup Ramen from the convenience store in front of the train station. I was an old hand at shoplifting, a skill I had picked up in junior high. An Extra-Large Cup Ramen was a difficult target, however: the package rustled, and its size made it hard to squeeze into my bag.

Shoplifting always leaves me feeling disappointed. It's not a "Damn, I've gone and done it again!" kind of thing. And it's not that I feel let down once the excitement of the moment has passed. Or even that I wish I had ripped off something more valuable. Rather, it's a vague, nonspecific form of disappointment.

From the convenience store, I hopped on my bicycle and pedaled back to the company apartments. There, waiting for me under the middle staircase, the one that leads up to my fifth-floor apartment, was a collapsible plastic box from the local Shoppers' Co-op. I'm a member of the Co-op. They deliver every Thursday. My order tends to draw attention because it's so skimpy—I might get only a bag of Co-op madeleines, or perhaps a jar of Co-op strawberry preserves. You could never act so dainty and refined, one of the housewives in the building told me, if you had children of your own. When my kids were in preschool, she went on, I loaded one child on the front of my bike, the other in the back, and then we wobbled down the street with five cartons of tissues and a jam-packed supermarket shopping bag in the front basket. That was how she explained it to me. I didn't say anything, just nodded in response.

We all call one another *okusan*. An *okusan* has blemish-free skin and muscular arms. She puts her Co-op order in a reusable bag and lugs it up to her apartment. I stuff my order—Co-op ketchup and Co-op mini donuts this time around—in my tote bag and trudge up the staircase. When I show the kitchen god what I bought, he snorts in disgust.

"Sweet stuff again, huh," he says.

I like sweets, it's true, but I like stucco even more. I boiled water for the Extra-Large Cup Ramen I had pilfered that morning. Stucco tastes great, but it doesn't fill me up. I then devoured the ramen, right down to the last drop of broth, polished off a whole bag of sugar-coated biscuits, stuffed six sticks of plum-flavored gum in my mouth, and clasped my hands in prayer to the kitchen god. My mother trained me to pray to him every morning, noon, and night. I heard him growl underneath the fridge. Then everything went quiet.

"OKUSAN!" CALLED a voice from behind me.

It was an *okusan* from the building next to mine. The one whose eyes were set very far apart. I thought that separation made her look cute. I like cute things. If it's sweet or cute, it's for me.

"Did you hear tell what's going on in the trash disposal area?"

Did I hear tell? I hadn't come across that phrase since I read *Little Women* when I was young. I shook my head.

"The crows are bad enough, but to make matters worse, now it seems we have a weasel."

I opened my mouth wide. "Oh, that's terrible," I said, opening my eyes wide as well.

"It looks like this," the *okusan* said. Hunching her back, she began running around in small circles.

"Oh, that's terrible," I said again. The *okusan* handed me a clipboard. As I'm in charge of looking after the staircases this year, it's my job to circulate all the relevant information to the residents, starting on the first floor: in addition to the circular, the clipboard has a sheet of paper with two columns, one column for me, listing in order the units I must call on, and a second column that the residents have to stamp with their seal.

The *okusan* tittered when I suggested that we trap the weasel and sell it. I thought she looked even cuter when she laughed. When I added that the weasel's pelt might be worth something, though, she stopped laughing and walked off with her nose in the air.

I decided to climb back up to my apartment to prepare the circular. The air inside was warm and humid. I watered the spider plants. They've been growing like crazy. I got the original cutting from the *okusan* who lives on the floor below me.

Living rooms that have potted spider plants, cyclamens, and philodendrons I call "aunts' living rooms." My mother's elder sister Aunt Katsura had big pots of those plants scattered around her living room, as did Aunt Nana, as did Aunt Arika. All three aunts also made sure to lay down small rugs in their front entranceways. Glass jars full of potpourri were placed on their bathroom shelves. Cowrie shells and glass figurines of horses graced their kitchen counters. At Christmastime, cards from abroad were lined up on top of the shoe racks in the entranceway.

I never felt comfortable in my aunts' homes. They were always patting me on the head and forcing chocolate chip cookies on me. None of their kitchens seemed to have a god in it, but once, when Aunt Arika slipped into her kitchen to add hot water to a pot of apple tea, I heard a squeaky voice through the crack in the door.

"Aunt Arika, is someone in your kitchen?" I asked when she came out.

"It's a weasel, Izumi," she replied with a smile. "A scary, scary weasel. If you go in the kitchen, it'll catch you and eat you up." She arched her eyebrows, the smile still frozen on her face.

"Is it an old weasel?" I asked, but all that earned me was another chocolate chip cookie.

My living room bore a slight resemblance to the living rooms of Aunt Arika and my other aunts, but without the sweet, cloying atmosphere that filled their homes. All my living room had was spider plants, pots and pots of them, with a little kitchen god scampering around in between. The *okusan* who lived below me, however, did have an aunt's living room, with cyclamens and philodendrons, as well as a yucca and a fragrant corn plant, called a "tree of good fortune." A rug sat in the front entranceway.

Was the weasel visiting the trash disposal area the same kind of weasel as the one in Aunt Arika's kitchen? I could feel my thoughts beginning to stray as I pondered this question. Alarmed, I joined my hands in prayer to the kitchen god. My mother had often warned me not to allow empty spaces to form in my mind. When that happens, she taught me, all kinds of bad things can sneak in. If you prayed to the kitchen god, however, he could drive those bad things away for you.

MR. SANOBE and I got together at a coffee shop called the Olive Tree, situated in the building above the train station.

I had been introduced to Mr. Sanobe by an *okusan* who lived in the building two down from mine. It seemed that he worked as a salesman of textbooks and other educational materials. He and I had gone to a hotel together three times. After each meeting, Mr. Sanobe had given me 25,000 yen.

"Why are you giving me money?" I had asked him.

"You know, your breasts are awesome," was his response. He never answered my question.

Right after our first meeting, when I was wending my way home with the extra 25,000 in my purse, I bumped into the same *okusan* from the building two down from mine in front of the station. She was carrying a tiny handbag. Too tiny to contain even the smallest coin purse.

"What a cool handbag," I said, whereupon she laughed and extracted from it a single small stone. It was white and smooth to the touch.

"Here, it's yours," she said.

"For me?" I asked. She nodded.

"Take good care of it."

"I will!" I answered.

"How was Mr. Sanobe?" the *okusan* asked.

"He gave me money," I said. Her eyes widened.

"Don't ever say that out loud," she said.

"Should I give it back?"

"No, it's just something that we have to keep to ourselves."

"O-oh, I see," I said laughing. She laughed with me. We walked back to the company apartments together, our steps matching. She was still laughing as she climbed the stairs to her apartment. I rolled the small white stone she had given me between my fingers for a moment. Then I tossed it in the gutter.

Mr. Sanobe was sipping his iced coffee in the Olive Tree. It was always iced coffee for that guy.

"How do you feel about me, Izumi?" he asked.

"I like you," I answered. "I think you're cute." I especially liked the way his hair was thinning in front.

"Does your husband have any idea what's going on between us?"

"No, none at all."

"Are you sure?"

"Let's go to the hotel," I said, rising from my seat. Mr. Sanobe followed right on my tail. I tried a few new things in our hotel room, stomping on him, slapping him around, and calling him some nasty names. He loved it. Before we left, he gave me 28,000 yen.

"I hope we can make this last forever, Izumi," he said, as we headed out the door.

"I hope so too," I replied.

"I want us to be lovers," he said immediately.

"What do you mean, lovers?"

"You know, going to movies together, taking trips, hanging out on the phone."

"Sure."

Mr. Sanobe gasped in surprise. "Well then, next time we'll meet as lovers. It's a promise, right?" His forehead was glistening as he took me in his arms. I kissed the sweaty skin with a loud smack.

I stopped by the flower store in the station on my way home and used the 28,000 yen Mr. Sanobe had given me to buy the biggest potted philodendron they had. There was still a lot of money left over, so I picked up a fancy box lunch with salmon roe and grilled salmon as well.

When I got home, I put the plant on the small table next to the living room window. Then I unwrapped the crinkly packaging of the box lunch and ate the contents. I picked off the grains of rice stuck to the box and the wooden cover and ate them too. The kitchen god came out from under the fridge and ran a quick circle around the table with the new plant on it. When I showed the god how clean the box and the wooden cover were, all three of his faces nodded in approval. I took a plastic cup of Co-op custard from the fridge. The only things left inside were beer, a bag of *oden* that I had stolen from the convenience store the week before, and four soft-boiled *onsen* eggs. I gave the god a bit of my custard. He sucked it up, sprinted around the spider plants, and disappeared under the fridge. I took a bath and immediately fell asleep.

HOW NICE to be childless—you stay so young, said the *okusan* who lived in the apartment kitty corner to mine on the floor below.

It's rare for a childless woman to be asked, Don't you want children? It's common, though, for a mother with one child to be asked if she intends to have a second.

I don't like the idea of "making" children anyway, my neighbor says from time to time. We are blessed with them, right? I mumble my assent and nod. That very morning, I had lifted a carton of milk and a plastic bottle of green tea from the convenience store. They made my tote bag so heavy I swore never to pilfer drinks again.

The *okusan* living kitty corner to me on the floor below came up beside me in the hallway. This week it was my turn to clean the trash disposal area, so I was walking along carrying an empty bucket, a dustpan, and a broom.

"That weasel is a serious problem," she said.

I hadn't seen the weasel myself. These days, though, it was a common topic of conversation for the *okusan* community in our company apartments. It's a lot worse than the crows, they complained. Ripping up garbage bags is bad enough, but squeezing through the mail slot to get into someone's apartment and then laying waste to the kitchen? That's another thing altogether. It's absolutely dreadful. Weasels invading our kitchens—how do you deal with something like that?

The *okusan* stood there leaning against the cinderblock wall next to the trash cans, chattering while I splashed buckets of water over the concrete floor.

"Have you ever seen the weasel?" I asked her.

"No, but don't you think it's a terrible situation?" she replied.

Come to think of it, I hadn't come across anyone who had laid eyes on the animal.

"I wonder if it really exists," I muttered, refilling my bucket with water from the hose.

"Weasels multiply like crazy, too," she went on, still leaning against the cinderblock wall.

She kept watching me as I went through the process of cleaning the area.

"How does the weasel find its way out of the kitchen once it has gotten inside?" I asked. The concrete I'd splashed with water was gleaming black.

"What are you doing about the storage problem in your kitchen?" she asked, ignoring my question. "There just isn't enough shelf space in these buildings, is there?" I described the long, narrow shelves designed for small spaces that I had purchased on line. She praised the equally narrow shelves she had bought that boasted an even greater storage capacity. I murmured a few "uh-huhs" and nodded.

"Does a god live in your kitchen?" I blurted out. What on earth induced me to mention the kitchen god to a near stranger that way? I myself have no idea. It just slipped out.

"It's so gross, leaving footprints all over the kitchen."

"What?"

"They eat fish right down to the bones, you know. And that's not all."

She was still talking about the weasel. I studied her face as I gathered up the cleaning tools. This *okusan* had a prominent nose. And she was as thin as a rail.

"Are weasels at all cute?" I asked her.

"Weasels can make themselves flat. There isn't a crack that they can't get through," she replied. I bowed in her direction and started up the steps. She returned the bow but continued to stand there, propped against the wall.

When I got back to my apartment, I asked the kitchen god if he'd seen a weasel, but he didn't make a sound. I clasped my hands and prayed to him—prayed and prayed, wiping all else from my mind.

MR. SANOBE phoned, hoping to get together. We met at our usual place, the Olive Tree, but when I started for the hotel, he tugged at my sleeve.

"Let's go to the game arcade," he said.

"What would we do at a game arcade?" I asked.

"You know, play games and stuff," he answered, sweat beginning to ooze from his forehead.

We walked for a while, turned down what looked like an alleyway, and there, sure enough, was a game arcade. Maybe because it was the middle of the day, no customers were inside. Mr. Sanobe won a stuffed animal playing the UFO Catcher game.

"What a cute dog," I said.

"It's a raccoon," he said. He gave it to me. I found

nothing at all cute about it, however. I crammed it into my handbag. Mr. Sanobe moved on to the car-driving game. I stood behind him watching until he crashed, for my benefit, it seemed.

"Aren't you going to give it a name?" he asked.

"Give what a name?"

"The raccoon."

"Oh," I muttered vaguely.

"Let's call him Peter," Mr. Sanobe chirped, after receiving no response from me. So, Peter it was. He kissed me, right there in the back of the arcade. Then we headed off to the hotel, where, like before, I gave him a good trampling.

"Do you ever think about divorce, Izumi?" he asked. We were in bed, and I was just drifting off to sleep.

"What?" I snapped. It was pure reflex.

"I love you, Izumi," he said, pulling me closer to him. "I really mean it."

I held my breath. I hate it when I'm lying down and someone slips an arm under my shoulder like that.

A few minutes later, Mr. Sanobe began to get dressed. I put on my bra and panties. We had already said goodbye, and I was shopping in the station building when it hit me—he hadn't given me money this time around.

I PLACED a pot of cyclamens in my living room. The red flowers seemed to strike a chord with the kitchen god. His sprints around the room became more frequent.

The *okusan* next door had just left. She'd stopped by for tea with a loaf of banana bread that she had baked herself. The banana bread wasn't very sweet.

"My, what a lot of green!" she exclaimed when she saw my apartment.

"Not all that much," I said.

She took a sip of tea. "It must take a lot of looking after," she went on.

"Not all that much," I repeated. The kitchen god came running into the room. He scampered about among the spider plants, philodendrons, and cyclamens.

"Green plants aren't easy, getting them to grow properly." Had she seen the kitchen god or not? She sounded a bit distracted. "My husband's home late every night and my children are busy with their own lives, so I was thinking maybe I'd take a course in gardening, but the children's expenses are going to keep mounting. I'd like to find work, but I'm afraid I'm too old," she said as she shoveled in the banana bread. I sat there and nodded.

"Don't you work?" she asked me.

"I'm not really qualified for anything," I replied. The kitchen god was racing madly around the spider plants. I was suddenly overcome by an urge to vomit. I held it back, though, and the feeling passed.

The *okusan* left not long after that. I plopped down on my kitchen floor and began munching the stucco. I tossed what remained of the banana bread in the garbage. The kitchen god circled the garbage can, sniffing its contents. I picked up the god and pressed my cheek to his. All three of his cheeks, I should say. It felt as though bad things were trying to steal into my mind, so I put the god down and began praying to him with all my might.

When I walked back into the living room, the thick,

musty smell of the potted plants rose to greet me. The plants blanketed the floor so tightly it was hard to move around. I edged my way to the table and placed the cups and dishes the *okusan* and I had used on a tray. I figured it was a good time to pedal over to the convenience store and shoplift something. I grabbed my tote bag and thumped down the stairs.

I BEGAN to get calls from Mr. Sanobe during the day. He phoned every hour, sometimes every ten minutes.

Every third call or so, he would say something along the lines of, "Is a man there with you?" and I would answer, "Fat chance," which would set him laughing. Then he would change the subject, and ask if I had seen the big home run on TV the night before, or tell me he was thinking of quitting his job.

"How is Peter?" he inquired. My memory was hazy, but I knew I had tossed the stuffed raccoon in the gutter at some point.

"I treasure the little guy," I answered. He laughed happily. Then he went into his, "I love you, Izumi, I really do," routine.

The *okusan* who lived in the building two down from mine, the one who introduced me to Mr. Sanobe, moved out. Apparently, she had purchased a custom-built home. The next time the Co-op delivery arrived, the *okusan* gathering around the boxes that held our orders gossiped about her. How could she have afforded such an extravagance? Weren't we in an economic slump? Bonuses had shrunk, right? Maybe she had inherited some money. She had all the luck!

We wasted no time dividing up our purchases. The wall of our building was turning gray, I thought, as I leaned over the rim of the plastic box. I could feel my mind beginning to wander. Alarmed, I tried to focus on a package of Co-op flour. Then I shifted to a box of the Co-op chestnut and bean paste sweets. If I could just keep focusing on external objects like those, I thought, then bad things couldn't sneak into my mind.

MR. SANOBE started asking if he could visit me at home.

"C'mon," he said on the phone one day. "Tell me where you live. Then I can come and visit."

I smothered a laugh. He fell quiet, waiting for an answer. I said nothing. The silence was driving him crazy—I could tell.

"You and I are lovers, right, Izumi?"

I hung up immediately.

After that, I stopped answering the phone altogether. Wordless messages were left on my answering machine, but those ended after a few days.

I went to the kitchen and began to peel small flakes of stucco off the walls.

"You shouldn't eat that stuff," the kitchen god warned me. The walls in the kitchen were turning dark. I had stripped off almost all the stucco. Underneath, the plaster surface was all gray and bumpy.

I went to the convenience store. An *okusan* followed me in. She wanted to talk, so I couldn't shoplift. When she finally left, another *okusan* took her place. The weasel was on her mind, so she gabbed on about that. Not long afterward, a third *okusan* showed up, also interested in the weasel situation. With all the talk about weasels, I had no chance to steal anything. I was going nuts.

Apparently, weasels were running rampant throughout our building complex. They were impossible to drive out, no matter how many times you hit them. They laid waste not just to kitchens but to everything—living rooms, bedrooms, nowhere was safe.

I was finally able to pilfer a pack of safety pins and leave the store. The sky was a cold, wintry blue. Wisps of cloud floated high overhead. My eyes were bleary, unfocused.

I went to the kitchen to pray to the kitchen god. Recently, I had been blanking out a lot, which meant it was easy for bad things to find their way in. I prayed and prayed to the god every day.

MR. SANOBE showed up.

I didn't have a chance to ask how he had found me, for the moment he closed the front door he pushed me down on my back right there in the entranceway.

I smiled sweetly at him. He wasn't looking at my face, though, but at the philodendrons, cyclamens, and spider plants, which had overflowed my living room and spilled into the entranceway. My head almost banged into a potted philodendron when he forced himself on me.

Mr. Sanobe finished up quickly and hurried out the door. When he left, he bowed and, in a loud voice, called out, "Please think it over, *okusan*. You will not be disappointed in the quality of our merchandise, I guarantee it."

I slammed the door and headed for my bedroom, skirting the living room and its wall-to-wall plants. I threw myself on the bed. The bedroom floor too was almost completely covered with potted plants. I fell asleep the moment my head hit the pillow.

When I awoke, I could see the winter sky outside my

window. The sun had gone down since Mr. Sanobe's visit, but night had not yet fallen. Something shot past the window. The weasel, perhaps? I went to the kitchen. The kitchen god was running around. All three of his faces looked angry. Taken aback, I clasped my hands and prayed. When I went to scrape some stucco off the wall, though, there was hardly any left— all I could manage were a few tiny bits. I leaned against the naked wall, my mind a blur.

"Are you happy?" the kitchen god asked.

The kitchen god was prone to ask out-of-the-blue questions of that sort. I sensed that my mind was vulnerable to bad things entering, so I prayed to him with all my might. Was I happy? I had never given that question a thought. My mind was growing more and more scattered. I knew that bad things could sneak in when I was in this condition, so I scrambled to focus on something. Since I wasn't sure what that something should be, though, I prayed with all my heart for the people in my life:

May Mr. Sanobe find happiness.

May my mother find happiness.

May Aunt Katsura find happiness.

May Aunt Nana find happiness.

May Aunt Arika find happiness.

May all the *okusan* find happiness.

The kitchen god scampered as I prayed. He circled the philodendrons, the spider plants, the cyclamens in their pots. Around and around, he ran.

Mole

THIS IS how my day begins.

I wake early—most mornings, before my wife.

If the sun is up, a faint light shines through the cracks in the ceiling. I lie there a while, gazing at the thin rays of sunshine entering the room.

On cloudy days, or if it's raining, no light enters. When it snows, which is rare, an almost imperceptible whiteness filters through, even before daybreak.

Under the covers is nice and warm, but the tip of my nose is cold. I'd like to use the toilet, but it's so cozy I have a hard time getting myself out of bed.

In the end, my wife is the one who gets up first. She's a creature of the morning, humming a tune as she bustles about lighting the kitchen stove and launching into the housework.

By the time I'm finally dressed and ready to go check on the humans I hauled in yesterday, or the day before, or the days before that, the stove is glowing red, the kettle is singing away, and the smell of toasting bread fills the room. My wife is quick on her toes, that's for sure.

The humans I picked up, they're all in the next room.

Most are sprawled on the floor. There is a generous supply of mattresses and pillows, blankets and quilts. Few ask for permission to use them. Some burrow in the moment they arrive. Some shove aside the humans who are already sleeping there to steal their place in the warm bedding. Some stomp about the room, trampling on those lying on the floor. They're all like that. After about half a day, though, each has marked out their own territory and the room has quieted down.

Every morning, I go about tapping each human on the shoulder. First, to make sure they're alive. Second, to see if they want to leave right away, or if they're going to stay for a while.

I drag those who have died to the pit and toss them in. The pit is even deeper than the hole we live in, at least a hundred meters to the bottom. I didn't dig it myself. Nor did my wife. It was our ancestors, generations of them, who scraped it out, bit by bit.

Its original purpose was as a receptacle for the dead of our own clan. As the years passed, however, our numbers steadily diminished until now the only ones of us left in this world are our parents and our younger siblings—a pair of sisters and a pair of brothers.

All of them, parents and siblings alike, moved far south, beyond Kyushu, to live in the deepest recesses of the earth. In that underground redoubt they can pass their days quietly, undisturbed by any human intruders. My wife's mother sends an email every so often, urging us to get out of Tokyo as soon as possible and join them. She seems to be afraid that our siblings will announce that they plan to follow us to Tokyo.

A simple tap on the shoulder tells me which humans can leave—those ready to go are able to respond. Humans in their condition always look helpless, forlorn. They catch my eye with theirs and mumble something unintelligible.

I pat their shoulder and smile. Then I go back to the living room and eat a breakfast of crispy bacon and yoghurt with peach jam.

When I have finished, my wife and I carry a sloshing tureen of her stew to the room where the humans are kept. She spoons the contents into wooden bowls, while I do my best to make them line up properly. Being human, though, many are too lazy to wait, so they cut into line or snatch their comrades' bowls. I warn them at first, but if they persist, I shout and slash at them with my claws until order is restored.

Once the stew is eaten, the room settles down again. I begin to prepare for work. My wife is scrubbing the sink while the washing machine chugs away. She sees me off as I raise the trapdoor to the outside world and step out onto the street. I stroll to the station in my cashmere coat and scarf. Not to mention my leather gloves. (I hate the cold.) I change trains twice, and arrive at my office in under an hour.

I stamp my time card and flip through the pile of faxes on my desk as I wait for one of the office ladies to bring my tea. When I first entered the company, I was often bullied— my fellow workers threw stones at me, pelted me with rotten food, that kind of thing—but in recent years everyone seems to have gotten used to me, fellow workers and bosses alike.

It doesn't seem to register with new employees how different I look. It's not that they're holding back from commenting; rather, it appears they're just not paying attention. Sure, someone might say, "My, but you're hairy!" every so often, but no one gawks anymore, or presses me to reveal who and what I am. Until ten years ago the gossips targeted me, but not these days.

I sit in front of my computer until noon, going over the figures. Every so often, a girl from General Affairs comes to ask me to use my brush to write an address in ink on an envelope. My penmanship is one of the things I am known for. In fact, it is said that my calligraphy is better than that of anyone else in the company.

I work away quietly, so that when I open the box lunch my wife has prepared, I've already finished my quota for the morning. The heat is on in the office, but I'm still cold, so I wrap a heating pad around my back and another around my lower abdomen. Once they're lukewarm, I know it's time to eat.

THIS IS how my lunch break goes.

When I finish eating my box lunch, I carefully wrap up the empty box, wash my paws, and scrub my face. I use chopsticks when I eat, but my palms and my claws participate as well. By the end, my paws are all sticky with grease, and bits of food cling to the fur around my cheeks and mouth.

Perhaps my office mates find my way of eating disgusting, or perhaps they simply don't want to hang around the office during their lunch break, but they make themselves scarce when I'm having my lunch—the only ones left in our section are me and the girl minding the telephone. So it's quiet, but also a bit chilly.

Too chilly for me, in fact, so once I finish my meal, I head down to the park next to the train station for the rest of my lunch hour.

Humans live there in cardboard boxes, a whole slew of them, so I choose the box that looks the warmest and ask to be admitted.

When I crawl inside, the man stares at me goggle-eyed. "You ain't human, is you?" he asks, looking me up and down, my face, my legs, the whole bit. The homeless inspect me far more thoroughly than my colleagues at work, no question.

"No, I'm not," I answer proudly, thrusting out my chest.

"Don't be so stuck up," the homeless man grins. "You're just a damned animal."

"And you're not? Humans are animals too, haven't you heard?"

"Yeah, I guess you're right."

This is the extent of our conversation. Homeless humans don't talk a whole lot. Neither do the sort of humans I pick up off the street. All in all, Tokyoites have turned into a pretty tongue-tied bunch.

I press my back against the back of the homeless man and, slowly, begin to heat up. This sure beats sitting in the cold office—come rain or snow, sitting back to back with a human is the best way to get warm. Yet humans don't do it very often, for whatever reason. Sometimes I find myself puzzling over why humans are so cold and distant with each other.

The humans I pick up are not the homeless ones. No, the ones I take home are far more unstable.

I leave the homeless man's cardboard box and head over to spend some time in the alleys that run behind the train station. Humans on their last legs don't choose alleys like this. They prefer more public spaces. Like the shops inside the station, or the well-lit, glass-walled coffee shop, or the department store.

Cats live in the alleys. When a cat sees me, the fur on its back stands on end, and it yowls. Humans have a soft spot for cats, so those yowls bother them a lot. I steer clear of cats as I walk the alleys.

When I reach the deepest recesses of an alley, I might come across a hole in the ground. If I curl up small and work my way inside, I strike soft earth. When that happens, I start digging away with my claws. I'm a good digger—when the spirit strikes me, I can tunnel all the way home. It drives my wife batty to see how dirty this makes my treasured cashmere coat. I just give her a kiss, and go back to my digging.

The sun is blinding when I return to the surface. On cloudy days as well, I have to close my eyes and wait for them to readjust. Even so, light penetrates my eyelids. It's a cold light. Yet it comes from the sun. My wife says that's because the distance between the sun and the earth's surface is too great. Since the magma at the earth's core is hot, though, it's warmer underground. The humans I pick up must find the room at my place a good deal warmer than what they are used to on the surface, given how well they sleep.

Once my eyes have adjusted to the point that I can open them, I brush the dirt from my coat, wrap my scarf around my neck, and return to the office. With everyone back from lunch, the place is jam-packed. I switch on my computer and download columns of figures from the database. One of the office ladies brings me tea. I pick up the cup in my paws and sip.

Sometimes the cup slips through my claws and shatters on the floor. When that happens, they sweep up the shards without a word. Not one glances at my face. In fact, no one in the office ever looks in my direction. They don't attempt to talk to me either.

I face my computer and type away, my claws clattering on the keyboard.

THIS IS what my afternoons are like.

My office warms a little in the afternoon sun. There are three rubber plants in pots lined up in the reception area. I blow the dust off their leaves on my way to the restroom. Those leaves are magnets for dust. A light coating forms in just half a day, the product of all the human activity.

I enter a restroom stall. I'm shorter than humans, just two-thirds the height of an average man, so I can't use the urinals. One time, I threw caution to the wind and tried, but that didn't go well at all—my pee bounced back and splashed all over me. No surprise there.

When I return from the restroom, I always make it a point to say hi to the maintenance staff. Most afternoons they're holed up on the emergency staircase, somewhere between the second and third floor. They're not talking—they're just standing around, leaning against the wall.

"Hey," they might say. "You should go check outside the building. One of them may be out there."

"One of them" means a human for me to pick up.

"This one looks a bit sketchy."

"How do you mean?"

"Like he might be fixing to jump off a roof or something."

"That sucks," the other workers chime in. "I saw a jumper take the dive once," someone says, and the group starts laughing and joking. Why in the world are they laughing? I have no idea. I'm not laughing. I laugh only when something makes me feel good. Humans are different, though—their laughter means something else. But what? Humans really stump me.

I pull out my notepad and jot down where I can find the "one."

Back at my desk, I turn to my computer as an office lady brings me tea. The tea we get after our lunch break is always lukewarm. Maybe that's because humans get tired in the afternoon. They should sleep, but instead they sit in chairs and walk around, their bodies constricted by their clothes.

If I get tired, whether I'm in the office or in the corridor, I lie down. I fall right to sleep wrapped in my cashmere coat, which serves as a blanket. The humans make a big circle to avoid me, though I've chosen the most out-of-the-way spot. Their shoes clatter more loudly than necessary as they pass, as if to signal how hard they are working.

When I wake from my nap, I'm chilled to the bone. That's what comes of sleeping directly on the floor, but what else can I do? I hop to my feet. For a second, I can sense the humans react. There's no obvious stir, but the air in the room changes. I can tell.

Humans loathe me. It's been like that forever. My ancestors would never have believed that one of their kind could live among humans, sharing their everyday life, as I am doing now. Humans hated the very sight of our race—if they glimpsed us, they grabbed a gun to shoot us, or a spade to crush us, or scattered poison to try and wipe us out. It was terrible.

Rare is the human who would choose to attack us now. Who do they hate, and who do they like? These days, such questions seem only to confuse them. In their heart of hearts, that original loathing lives on; yet they are willing to accept my presence at the office. They convince themselves that I am somehow essential to the company, so they accept me. In fact, however, practically no one needs us. As far as most humans are concerned, we who live in the bowels of the earth are agents of darkness, nothing more.

I can hear the unfriendly murmurs as I walk slowly back to my desk, sit again before my computer, and accept the cup of lukewarm tea from the office lady. When I check my inbox, I find a batch of messages from people who have spotted the ones I am looking for in such and such a place. I jot down the locations in my notebook and delete the emails.

My emails are increasing day by day. The mutterings of those who have heard of my activities advance in my direction, seeking to enter the cracks, like slender roots that work their way into a boulder until it splits.

I drink the lukewarm tea, and drop the cup on the floor. On purpose this time. Humans are so filled with loathing, yet so lacking in ways to let it out. They just sweep up the shards of my shattered cup, while the dark cloud hovering over them grows even darker.

I study the numbers on my computer, acting as though nothing has happened. The sun is setting outside the big windows, suffusing our office in a pale red light. Soon the color covers the whole sky. A Tokyo sunset, all-encompassing, the sky dyed a fierce red.

In my notebook, I start making a list of all the ones I will be picking up after work, and the order in which I will pick them up.

THIS IS how I spend my evenings.

I always give a long, deep bow from the waist when I leave the office. In the gathering dusk, the building's walls appear wet, its outline indistinct. The light pouring through the windows makes them look like empty sheets of paper suspended in the air. My human co-workers give my bowing form a wide berth as they pour out onto the street. They never turn to look back at their workplace. Although return would be impossible were they to die in the night. Instead, they rush out and hurry home.

When I have fully completed my bow, I set out for the city streets.

Night is still shallow. The darkness faint.

I enter an izakaya and order a draft beer. At first the young waiter is discombobulated by how hairy I am, but he hides it well, calling out my order with no change of expression. An accompanying dish of shredded white radish simmered in mirin and soy sauce follows soon after.

The young waiter's initial surprise quickly vanishes. One after another, he brings me my orders—lightly fried tofu in broth, grilled and salted chicken gizzards, poached yellowtail and white radish.

I am working on my second carafe of warm sake when I ask him, "Any of them around these parts?"

"No, they don't show up in a place like this."

Yet a quick scan of the room tells me that, in fact, a couple are there. One has cloudy eyes and looks utterly exhausted; the other's eyes are a clear blue, and his head slumps on his chest. The young waiter utterly ignores them, bustling briskly about the place as if he hadn't heard their orders.

The two of them slide off their chairs and start to stagger around, occasionally banging into the walls. I deftly snatch them up, hooking their backs with my claws. I let each dangle there for a few moments while they shrink to half my size and then even smaller, so that, finally, they can fit in my palm.

At that point, I slip them into the pockets of my cashmere coat. They go quietly without a peep of protest. As if this is what they want.

"Your bill is 3,500 yen," the young waiter says when I'm done.

"You had a few of these," I say, plucking one from my pocket and dangling it in front of him. His eyes widen with surprise.

"So, they were here after all," he says with a shrug. "What are they anyway?" he asks. I can see that he is spooked by the tiny thing, which is too exhausted to open its eyes.

"I don't know myself, yet still . . ." I reply.

Yet still? The young waiter is waiting for me to go on, but I return the thing to my pocket and reflect for a moment. Over the last ten years, these things have increased in number. When dealing with despair, my parents' generation used to say: "I've lost the spirit to live." Maybe they are humans who have likewise lost the energy to stay alive.

If left alone, they hollow out. First, they themselves, then the place where they stand, then ultimately the entire area around them empties. All real substance is lost.

But this does not mean they are dead.

Apparently, dying requires actual strength.

Unable to live, unable to die, they're just there, eating away at their surroundings. Eating away at themselves. That is who they are.

When did the first one come tumbling into our home? There was a loud thump, I recall, and when I went to investigate, I found him in the adjoining room. A human I had never seen before. At the time, my wife and I were living a quiet life in our underground world, quite free from any interactions with humans.

"I'm scared," the human said.

"What are you scared of?" my wife and I asked together.

"Everything," he said, staring blankly into space.

At first, one dropped into our home about every week, then every five days, then every three days, until it reached the point where at least one a day was making an appearance.

At first, all we had to do was wait. They would remain in the adjoining room for a while and then return to the surface.

"Going back?" we would ask.

"Yes," most would reply. It seemed they just needed a short spell underground to be able to return.

All kinds of humans dropped in that way. Gangly youths, doddering old folks, adults in their prime. None were talkative; all were enfolded in the desolate air of above ground, which clung to them like skin.

If they died, my wife and I dug separate holes to bury them. Eventually, though, we remembered the pit our ancestors had excavated, and started tossing them in there. The bodies of dead humans are cold and stiff. Moles are no different—we grow cold and stiff when we die too.

Humans cry over the bodies of their fellows, though, while we don't. We only cry when we are sad or vexed about something. Death is a natural part of our world, so we see no reason to get sad. Or vexed. Humans are normally uncommunicative, empty, and apathetic; yet when one dies, the adjoining room shakes with all the weeping and sighing. They cry as though crying makes them feel good. Humans are impossible to understand.

I began picking them up a few years ago, collecting those who in their weakness had collapsed, and putting them in my pockets. Since I began doing that, my nights have become a whirlwind of activity. I write down the order I should follow in my notebook and then make my rounds. They basically remain in one place, so it's easy to snag them.

I spend half the night like this, never resting, picking up one human after another and stuffing them in the pockets of my cashmere coat.

LET ME tell you about my nights.

Gathering all those humans has worn me out.

I walk home along the black stretch of pavement, careful to stifle the clickety-clack of my shoes. My pockets are full to the brim with humans. I tap the outside of each pocket lightly every so often to make sure none have tumbled out.

When I arrive home, I raise the trapdoor and climb down inside. My wife is there waiting for me. I've told her she doesn't have to stay up, but she says dozing off and then waking again ruins her sleep, so she sips a cup of cocoa or hot milk as she waits, a sweater pulled over her pajamas.

"Welcome home," she greets me warmly. She has a gentle, sweet voice for a mole. Her whole family is like that. My father-in-law and brother-in-law speak softly, while my mother-in-law and sister-in-law sound exactly like my wife. Their faces aren't so similar, though.

How about a nice warm bowl of *ochazuke*, she asks, moving behind me to take off my cashmere coat and hang it up.

The coat's pockets are bulging. She reaches inside and extracts the humans with her claws: one, two, three, she counts, lining them up on the table.

The humans don't move at first. Eventually, though, the stronger ones begin to rustle about. As their movements become livelier, they start reverting to their original dimensions. When they're big enough, my wife and I carry them to the adjoining room, where they can complete their growing.

Those already in the room watch blankly as tiny humans transform into full-sized humans before their eyes. Most humans who end up here are, as a rule, no less foggy-headed. That fogginess seems to be their unvarying state of mind—they never seem able to focus, however unnatural or peculiar what they are seeing happens to be. Only when one of them dies do they show their feelings. Then, they blubber and moan.

When we have finished disposing of the humans, my wife and I sit across from each other at the table with hot cups of *hojicha* tea. We may nibble a rice cracker or two as well. Seldom do we mention the humans. Or my job. Instead, we talk about what the specials were at the supermarket. Or about the puppies born to Chiro, the dog who lives at the pharmacy. How, since their birth, Chiro has taken to barking madly when my wife passes. Those are the sorts of things we discuss while we sip our tea.

We can hear a stir in the adjoining room as the humans burrow between the mattresses and blankets. They may even exchange words. By putting our ears to the wall that divides the two rooms, we can sometimes make out what they are saying. Their voices are gentle. That's true of the humans who have fallen into the room as well as those I have picked up. Gentle. No one could call my office co-workers' voices gentle, though. Quite the opposite.

"It's so scary," the humans say.

"So scary . . . The ferns at the eaves," another said.

We have no idea what they're talking about. The humans I pick up sound like broken machines—their words make no sense. They just keep repeating "scary, scary," and moaning away.

"Scary" is the word they use most often. But what are they afraid of? With their foggy-headed expressions they go on endlessly repeating "scary, scary," to each other in those gentle voices. But what the hell is it that they find so scary? If it's that threatening, why can't we see the fear in their faces? I really don't understand humans.

My wife and I check the adjoining room before we go to bed. We engage in small talk with the humans: "Nice hat," we'll say, or "What's your favorite food?" or "Did you get a quilt? Oh, good." Their responses are surprisingly clear. Even though they're practically incapable of conversing with each other. "I like fish," one will say, "especially rock cod, so I went fishing, but this white, black, and brown striped cat showed up while I was sitting there, and, you know, I once killed a cat and ate it, but it tasted pretty awful.' This kind of nonsense spills out once they start talking.

Not long after that, my wife and I crawl into bed and drift off immediately.

In the adjoining room, the sighs and cries continue throughout the night. The noise used to keep us awake, but we've grown used to it.

My wife snores a bit. It seems I snore more loudly once I'm fast asleep.

LET ME tell you about the dawn.

Daybreak is the time of day when moles bear their children.

My wife has given birth to fifteen children so far. They were all small, hairy, and full of life. Yet all died soon after they were born. Not a single one survived. With great care, we buried each in its own hole.

The humans began to cry when they heard our baby had died. Some carried on even more than when one of their own passed away. My wife and I didn't cry, though. Death is part of the natural order, even when it strikes a newborn. Some humans I'd collected had strangled their own babies; yet they were the ones who moaned the loudest and thrashed around the most. Humans always perplex me.

It's not just moles—humans also tend to bear their young at daybreak.

Two of our humans have given birth in the last ten years or so. One baby was a boy, the other a girl. Both were small, hairy, and full of life. They may have been human, but they were the spitting image of baby moles. The humans looking on, however, showed no interest in them at all. Humans wail mightily when a death occurs but don't give a fart when it's a birth.

The two mothers took one look at their hairy babies and tossed them aside. Then they crawled under the covers and went back to sleep. When they returned aboveground a couple of days later, they left their babies behind. Humans just can't appreciate babies covered with hair. No exceptions.

My wife and I stepped in to raise the abandoned children. Both sprouted claws and grew to full maturity in just three years, much more rapidly than any of their human kinfolk. At that point, we set them free to live on the surface, whereupon they ran off somewhere. Neither has been heard of since.

When the sun comes up, a faint light shines through the cracks in the ceiling. I lie there a while, gazing at the thin rays of sunshine entering the room. On cloudy days, or if it's raining, no light enters. When it snows, which is rare, an almost imperceptible whiteness filters through, even before daybreak.

Under the covers is nice and warm, but the tip of my nose is cold. I'd like to use the toilet, but it's so cozy I have a hard time getting myself out of bed. In the end, my wife is the one who gets up first. She's a creature of the morning, humming a tune as she bustles about lighting the kitchen stove and launching into the housework.

By the time I'm finally dressed and ready to go check on the humans I hauled in yesterday, or the day before, or the days before that, the stove is glowing red, the kettle is singing away, and the smell of toasting bread fills the room.

The adjoining room is overflowing with humans. I drag the dead ones out and dump them in the pit, then quickly divide the rest into those who appear ready to return to the surface and those who don't. Then my wife and I dole out the stew she has prepared.

The humans are bereft of energy—their faces are lifeless. Yet they are not dead. They live by eating away at their surroundings, at themselves, without ever moving. They remain with us in our hole without ever becoming moles themselves, waiting for the time when, still human, they can return to the world aboveground.

Many die before they can return, whereupon their comrades wail and thrash about. That is the one time when their faces glow, even if only for a brief while.

The Roar

I GREW up suckling at the breast of my eldest sister, Ichiko.

I had seven older sisters. They were all beautiful—the napes of their necks, their heels, their breasts. Still, Ichiko's breasts were exceptional. Though she was not yet twenty, they were firm and full—tiny pale blue veins crisscrossed their immaculate whiteness, and when I sucked, what seemed an endless supply of milk came gushing out.

I preferred Ichiko's milk to my own mother's, which created a distance between us. My eyelashes had not yet grown in when I began spending all my nights and days in Ichiko's bed. I learned to crawl, then to walk, but still I showed no sign of wanting to leave that bed. The two times of day I ventured outside were at dusk and just before daybreak, when the light was dim, and objects wavered in the air. Then I would slip out of bed, open the shoji, and step down from the veranda. Once the soles of my feet hit the dirt, I would go skipping about the dark yard, which was hemmed in on all four sides by a dense grove of beech trees, while a beaming Ichiko looked on. Aa-chan, she would call out to me happily, you're such a good boy, the best. Buoyed by her words, I skipped even faster, faster than seemed humanly possible.

When darkness fell or the sun rose in the sky, I scampered up to the veranda and back into Ichiko's bed. Wringing out a cloth, Ichiko carefully wiped the dirt off my feet. Then she licked the soles with her tongue to cleanse them. All that hard exercise had set my blood racing, so I sucked her firm breasts even more greedily than usual, gulping as I drank. By the end, her breasts were drained and soft.

Ichiko and I slept curled together, like two magatama beads. We slept deeply, and long. At times, I would wake during the day to find her no longer beside me. Instead, she would be in a corner of the room, munching on a piece of meat. A platter of raw meat sat directly on the tatami and I could hear her chomping away, though her back was to me.

Ichiko could always tell when I was waking up. She would slowly turn to me and grin, strips of meat dangling from her mouth. When her lips parted, I could see small bits sticking to her perfectly straight teeth.

When she needed to use the toilet, Ichiko would pick me up and take me with her. Half dreaming, half awake, I would feel her hands under my knees as she suspended my bottom over the porcelain receptacle. When I had finished, she would squat and do her business. From deep below came a plop, followed by a sucking sound. I listened through ears dulled with sleep. Crouching in the darkness under the sink in the hall, I waited outside the open door until she'd finished. Ichiko carefully wiped herself, then hoisted me on her back and carried me back to our still-warm bed. In a matter of moments, both of us were fast asleep again.

Ichiko nursed me until I was five years old. Because I subsisted solely on breast milk, my bones were thinner than those of other children my age, and my complexion was disturbingly pale. I only came to realize this much later, though, since as long as I was breastfeeding I met no other children. I spent all that time in Ichiko's bed, enraptured.

IT WAS my second elder sister, Futaba, who dragged me from that bed.

Futaba was always blowing a small bird whistle that went *churichurichururu*. I could hear it from the room where I lay, warbling at the far reaches of the corridor. And then, almost immediately, would come the faint flapping of wings. A great flock of birds was on its way.

One day, I awoke in the middle of the afternoon, unusual for me. Ichiko was fast asleep, and I was nuzzling her breasts. It was bright outside; light filtered through the shoji and splashed across the tatami. I could hear the sound of the bird whistle and beating wings coming up the corridor: *churichuri*.

I crept out of bed and cracked open the shoji ever so slightly. I could see Futaba walking toward me. Actually, all I could see of her was her legs and torso, for her head and shoulders were covered with small birds. The birds were brightly colored—blue, yellow, and green predominated— some swirling about her face, others perching on her shoulders and arms.

A scattering of fallen feathers lay in Futaba's wake. I crawled out to the corridor and began picking them up. Scouring the passageway, I was able to gather several dozen, which I bunched together to make a kind of bouquet. The moment Futaba stopped blowing her whistle, the birds all flew away.

"You're Ichiko's kid, aren't you?" she asked me.

"No, I'm not," I answered, clutching my bouquet of feathers.

"Well, whose then?"

"I don't know."

Futaba laughed as if to mock my stupidity. Then she

wheeled and walked away. Alarmed, I hurried after her. Whenever a feather fell from my tiny hands, I stopped to pick it up. Futaba walked fast. It was all that I could do to keep from losing sight of her. The corridor was full of twists and turns, a real labyrinth. I followed her for hours, stopping each time she paused to decide which turn to take. From time to time, she would come to a halt and blow on her whistle, whereupon a flock of birds would stream out of the beech trees surrounding the yard and fly around her head. When the whistle went quiet, the birds all returned to the trees, as if being swallowed up. For a second, they mingled together there, a scattering of blues, yellows, and greens in the upper branches. The next instant, they were sucked into the dark treetops, and those colors disappeared. They must have been sucked very deep indeed.

The sun was setting when we finally reached Futaba's room. The lights were brightly lit, and there were signs of people everywhere. When Futaba slid open the shoji, the children in the room all turned to look at her.

"I'm back," she greeted them.

"Welcome home," they answered as one.

"I brought along a new kid," she said, nodding in my direction. The children swarmed around me. Their bodies gave off a warm, childish odor that made me grimace.

"He's small, isn't he?" they whispered to each other. "So pale!" "His eyebrows haven't grown in." "His hair's a shaggy mess." "He's got no clothes on!"

The children had me hemmed in on all sides; I had no room to breathe. How I longed to run back to Ichiko's bed. But navigating that long, twisting corridor was beyond me—no way could I manage that. The children combed my tangled hair and dressed me in clothes that fit, so that I had the appearance of a proper child. Then mealtime was called, and Futaba and the children gathered around a big table and began to eat. Some children served the food, others cleaned up afterward. When they were finished, a piece of paper was placed in front of each child, and everyone settled down to practice writing with a brush. After that came playtime, games like tossing a ball back and forth or playing war. Their shrill voices made me recoil. I had never stayed up so late before, and couldn't keep my eyes open. Following Futaba's instructions, the children laid out a straw pallet for me. The straw made me itchy, back, front, all over. I could see the children playing and quarreling from where I lay. Surrounded by their shrieks and laughter, lying on the straw, I fell asleep at last.

I DID get used to living with other children, though.

It turned out I had the shrillest voice of all. I hadn't used it before, so even I was taken aback when it burst from my body.

About twenty children lived in Futaba's room. There were some comings and goings, however. The child I grew closest to was a big boy with a mangled ear. He showed up not long after my arrival. The kids dubbed him One Ear. The name they gave me was Peewee, since I was so small. Peewee. One Ear. We grew to be close friends, calling each other by those nicknames. Whether it was cleaning up after meals or practicing calligraphy, we were always together. I stood out because of my loud voice, One Ear because he could pee farther than anyone else. We slept side by side on the same straw pallet. Sometimes I would wake at night to find his heavy arm draped over me. One Ear, I would gasp, I can't breathe. Still half-asleep, he would groan and remove it.

Every so often, Futaba threw a fit. She would take a long ruler and go around whacking kids on the arm or bottom with it. One Ear caught Futaba's eye because he was so big, so he came in for more than his share of whacks. He just glared coldly back at her. That made her whale on him all the harder.

One Ear and I had a secret hideaway, a place that was just our own. If we stepped down from the veranda, circled the thick stand of rushes, and crossed the barren stretch of sodden ground on the other side, we would come to a small pond. This "pond" was little more than a puddle grown big. No plants or living creatures lived there; only the occasional water strider skimmed its surface. A narrow stream of water seeped from the pond. I guess there must have been a spring feeding it from below. That stream trickled through the underbrush of the beech grove. Sometimes it seemed to disappear, but it always popped up again a little farther along. Deep within the trees it suddenly increased in size until it became a waterfall, spilling over the cliff on the far side of the grove.

None of the other kids knew a waterfall was there. In fact, the other children never ventured into the trees, not a single one. All we had to do when One Ear and I wanted to be alone was slip out the door when Futaba wasn't looking and take off for the waterfall.

Its water tasted sweet. We would be out of breath from all the running, but still One Ear and I scooped up the water in both hands and drank it. I call it a cliff, but it really wasn't that big. Scrambling through vines and over rocks to the very bottom posed no problem for us. One Ear taught me that the deep pool at the foot of the falls was called a basin.

"When I was born," he said, "I was given my first bath in a basin like that. How about you, Peewee?"

"I don't know," I replied.

That was the only answer I could give. I knew absolutely nothing. Not even the face of my own mother. Until the day that I went running after Futaba, my whole world had been Ichiko. I didn't know my own name. I didn't know why I had been born into this world. I had no idea what would become of me.

"They call a waterfall 'the roar' where I grew up," One Ear said.

"The roar."

"Not a little guy like this. No, I'm talking about the roar that seems to fall from heaven. More than a few waterfalls like that in the mountains."

"Why did you leave your hometown, One Ear?"

He didn't answer.

"They gave me my first bath in the biggest basin of all."

That's why he could bear up under Futaba's beatings, he went on. He glanced down and scooped up another handful of water.

One day, as she was whaling away, One Ear reached up with a big palm, grabbed the hand that was holding the ruler, and twisted it hard. Futaba's anger knew no bounds: she looked the very incarnation of wrath. She beat One Ear all the more furiously. In the end, his body was so swollen he couldn't get up. I spent the whole night tending to him as he lay stretched out, groaning on our straw pallet. One after another, I soaked compresses in an herbal infusion and laid them on his bruises. The treatment worked—by daybreak the swelling was gone, and he was as good as new. He sat up abruptly, gathered his few possessions, and prepared to make his departure.

"I'm leaving," he said, giving me a quick hug.

"For good, right?" I asked. He nodded.

"You've got a wiener, Peewee, so eat a lot and grow as big as you can." Now it was my turn to nod.

When the sun was up, One Ear set off through the yard. I saw him off as far as the waterfall. The beech trees were rustling in the breeze. Just once, One Ear looked back and gave me a wave. Then he was swallowed by the thick stand of trees.

SEVEN YEARS I spent there, at Futaba's. I made no more close friends after One Ear left. I did as he had told me, though, eating everything I could lay my hands on. Meat of uncertain origin, weirdly iridescent stewed fish—whatever was placed before me I crunched up, bones and all, and swallowed. When a pile of boiled uncut vegetables was served, I chewed them down to the core. I grew and grew until, before I knew it, I had passed Futaba in height. By that time, I was the old-timer of the group, the kid who had been there the longest. Futaba began to rely on me for things like overseeing the children's studies and keeping an eye on those who served and cleaned up after meals. Sometimes, she even let me blow on her bird whistle. When she used the whistle, countless small birds gathered, whereas my whistling attracted much larger birds.

One day, I was blowing on the whistle on the veranda

when the biggest bird I had ever seen flew up to me. Deftly, it grabbed me with its talons and carried me high into the sky. Those talons were razor sharp, yet my body was unharmed. The grove of beech trees grew smaller and smaller as the bird ascended, until we had soared so high it was just a black dot, where no branch or leaf could be made out. The Residence, its yard, the surrounding grove of beech trees, everything had become jumbled together, then reduced to a single point. The bird cut through the wind with a great swoosh. We crossed continents. We passed the dividing line between night and day. On and on we sped, until we came upon an island in the sea. The bird swooped down again and released me. I fell. As I tumbled, the familiar beech grove came into view. The top branches of a tree broke my fall. When I had clambered down to the ground, a woman I had never seen before was waiting for me. It was my third elder sister, Mitsue.

Mitsue was a funny sort of woman. Her moods, if you can call them that, were in constant flux. One day she would lord it over me, forcing me to massage every corner of her body— not just her legs and back, either—until my fingers became stiff and numb. Then the next day she was so attentive that she would warm my underwear against her chest. When I told her I didn't like her doing things like that, she wept silently and then vomited up a stream of small coins from her mouth. It was her habit to disgorge all sorts of things when something upset her.

One sweltering summer day, Mitsue was kneeling beside me, sending a cool breeze in my direction with a large fan. She had begun fanning me that morning, the moment I sat down at my desk to read. A number of tall bookshelves were lined up in the corridor outside Mitsue's room. On them sat countless volumes, old and new. I spent my days poring over Mitsue's books. When I asked if she had read them all, she responded with an ambiguous movement of her head, a nod that could have been taken as either yes or no. Yes, I've read them, she said after a pause, but I can't remember anything in them. A moment later, without warning, she opened the front of her kimono and out popped a breast. There was no rhyme or reason to the things she did.

Mitsue fanned me all that day—even when noontime came around, she refused to budge from her spot on the floor. I could feel my neck and shoulders on that side growing stiff from the constant breeze. In fact, that whole side of my body had grown completely rigid. Yet I feared what might come out of Mitsue's mouth if I disturbed her. The time before, it had been jellyfish. She had vomited up a number of the transparent creatures, all very much alive, right on the tatami. Wasting no time, we filled a big earthenware pot with water, and set them loose in it. Two are still alive. The rest apparently dissolved in the water.

Mitsue was half-naked. Plying the fan with such total concentration was making her sweat. A rivulet was coursing between her beautiful breasts. I found myself troubled by a strange and unfamiliar feeling. Shall I make some lunch? I asked. She nodded. I went to the kitchen, boiled some green vegetables, and whipped up some fermented soybeans. Mitsue kept fanning me the whole time, following me to the kitchen and standing beside me as I stood at the sink chopping vegetables.

I put our lunch on a tray and carried it to the table. Let's eat, I said. You've fanned me long enough. But she wouldn't stop. The food will get cold, I coaxed her. Fanning just cools it down. I could see my entreaties were falling on deaf ears. I'm getting cold, I said at last. Give it a break, won't you? This seemed to fluster her. She knitted her eyebrows and began pacing the room in her half-dressed state. Then she disgorged something.

This time, it was a small dragonfly bead made of colored glass. With green and white stripes. Still shaken, Mitsue picked it off the floor and squeezed it in her fist. Then, bead still in hand, she took her chopsticks, shoveled some fermented soybeans on her rice and stirred them together. In the process, the dragonfly bead fell on the tatami. She and I reached down to pick it up at precisely the same moment, so that our upper bodies pressed together. The sensation of her breasts against my shoulder gave me a massive erection. I pushed her on her back on the tatami and buried my face in those breasts. Stop it! she cried, but I couldn't stop. I could see the dragonfly bead on the floor. Stop it, stop it! Mitsue cried a few more times. Then she fell silent.

My face had worked its way down to Mitsue's navel when I felt things landing on my neck. Cold and clammy things. Whatever they were began slapping against my neck and shoulders. Alarmed, I jumped up, and they fell to the tatami. Salamanders, vomited up from Mitsue's mouth. My erection withered away to nothing.

Mitsue went on a while longer, disgorging more salamanders in her agitation. Some clustered around the dragonfly bead while others scampered under the chest of drawers, but by evening they had all crawled down into the yard in search of a moister place. Mitsue was quick to recover. I apologized for my behavior, and she nodded.

Three years I spent in Mitsue's room. When I announced my departure, what she vomited up that last time were lotus seeds. I placed the seeds in the amulet pouch she had sewed for me. It also contained the dragonfly bead. The seeds rattled when they came into contact with the bead. When we said goodbye, Mitsue took her breasts from her kimono and swung them back and forth as a token of our parting. I had not touched them since the salamander episode. They moved beautifully. I stared at them for a few moments, then turned and walked out. I looked back twice. Her breasts still swayed, and there was a sad expression on her face.

I WANDERED down the corridor, no particular destination in mind, until a light came into view in the distance. Once I passed Mitsue's bookshelves, the corridor became dark. At first, there was a faint glow behind me, but, before long, all was pitch black, so black I couldn't see the tip of my own nose.

I proceeded with one hand against the wall. Once in a while, one of my feet would step on the other. I jumped in alarm each time that happened.

The light ahead reminded me that I had eyes. That's how dark it had been. It was shining through a crack in the fusuma. Only a single ray, but more than enough to allow someone emerging from utter darkness to see. I ran to the fusuma and opened it.

Two identical women were seated on cushions, facing me. They were the picture of calm, as if I had somehow been expected.

"My name is Shima," said one.

"Mine is Goma," said the other.

I asked if they were twins, and they nodded together.

"Yes, we're twins, your fourth and fifth elder sisters," they chimed in unison.

I missed Mitsue's room already. Shima and Goma looked like crystal dolls. Not a single hair was out of place, and their voices cut like knives. No way did I want to live with them. Quietly, I took hold of the fusuma, intending to slide it open and make a run for it, but in that split-second, and with unanticipated speed, Shima, still kneeling on her cushion, flew to stay my hand. Goma circled to the other side and pressed down on my feet with her cushion.

"That will never do," Shima intoned solemnly.

"You are to remain here with us while you learn the workings of the world," Goma said, not to be outdone.

It took me an entire year to escape the clutches of Shima and Goma. Their training was rigorous and centered around two things: how to make unimpeachable apologies and how to flawlessly reprimand others. My apologies had to elicit tears from either Shima or Goma; my reprimands too had to make them cry from remorse. Otherwise, I had no hope of graduating from their instruction. Let me tell you, that instruction was strict!

One day, they let their guard down, and I was finally able to escape. I had never felt any closeness to them, not even for a moment. I flew down the corridor, pausing only when the light from their room was no longer visible. The amulet pouch was hanging around my neck, and I could hear the rustle of the dragonfly bead and the rattling of the lotus seeds.

The corridor stretched on and on, straight as an arrow. It never forked, nor were there any turns. I ran all day and all night until I arrived at Mutsumi's room.

Mutsumi was my sixth elder sister, the one who became my wife.

MUTSUMI WAS always distracted, her head in the clouds.

Her room was an absolute mess. An incense burner was perched atop a scattered pile of love letters from various men. A rice bowl studded with desiccated grains of rice overflowed with pills.

Our married life began the very day of my arrival. Mutsumi lay down on the mattress she left out on the floor and called me to her side as if it was the most natural thing in the world. Then we made love as if that was equally natural.

It was my first time, so I was in heaven. From morning till night, I entered Mutsumi's body at will. Mutsumi didn't seem to mind, letting me do whatever I wanted, but I could tell that her mind was elsewhere.

Mutsumi would disappear from time to time. Sometimes she would be gone three days, but it could take as long as a month for her to return. How I yearned for her there in that chaotic room.

Where have you been, I would ask when she got back. But she would never answer. If I pressed her hard, she might shrug and say she'd been visiting her sisters. I sure didn't want to talk about Shima and Goma, so that was the end of that conversation.

It was by sheer accident that I discovered she'd been visiting a man, and not Shima and Goma. She always chose the early afternoon to make her sudden departures, a time when I was taking my nap. I would open my eyes and she would be gone. It was that strange time of day when the air distorts things, so when I realized I had been abandoned there in her room it would feel terribly lonely. So lonely, in fact, that I would have another big erection, which made me feel even lonelier. All I could do was roll over and go back to sleep.

On this occasion, however, it seems I slept less deeply than usual. I heard Mutsumi trying to slip quietly out of the room. I opened my eyes and called her name, but there was no answer. I could hear her pace quicken when she reached the corridor. I jumped up and took off after her. For a while, Mutsumi followed the corridor toward Shima and Goma's, but eventually she drew to a halt and stepped down. She cut across the yard, and entered the grove of beech trees. I followed after, taking care to make my steps as quiet as possible. A foul sweat was seeping from my armpits and back. Mutsumi walked at a regular pace—I could tell that she had taken this path before. She entered the solitary house that stood at the end of the path. I circled around to the back to see what I could find. I heard Mutsumi's voice inside. A man's voice as well. The voices rose and fell, and continued for a long time.

I remained hidden behind the house for five days, observing the two of them, and how they lived. I gnawed at handfuls of grass when hungry. I ate insects too. I felt I had become a child of the undergrowth, a strange, ragged creature. Mutsumi appeared to be taking this relationship a lot more seriously. She was keeping the house tidy, and her conversations sounded more forthright and sustained.

I returned to Mutsumi's room on the sixth day, totally

down in the dumps. When I got there, I collapsed on the tatami without bothering to remove my filthy clothes. I don't know how long I slept, but when I awoke there was Mutsumi, snoring away on the bedding left out on the floor.

Where have you been, I grilled her. She sighed in her sleep. I slapped her face, and she woke. She looked vacantly up at me. I hit her. Her expression didn't change. Don't see that man anymore! I told her. She looked at me awhile. There was nothing in her gaze, no anger, no plea.

That's not how things are, she said simply and closed her eyes. Before long she was snoring peacefully again.

Mutsumi and the man seem to have ended their relationship soon after that, but it didn't take long for her to find another lover. I tried moving out, but I didn't have the nerve. I just couldn't leave her. I scattered the lotus seeds I had received from Mitsue in a pond within the beech grove. The next year, lotus shoots appeared in the water and, a few years later, flowers.

The flowers were large and pure white. They bloomed only when Mutsumi was off visiting some man or other. It would happen in the light of early dawn—I could actually hear the blossoms opening. I would walk to the edge of the pond to catch that sound. Standing there in the dark, I would wait for day to break with bated breath so as not to miss it. When the sun first brushed the tops of the beech trees, the buds swelled almost imperceptibly. Has the time come? I would wonder. Then the air around the buds would begin to shimmer, and the next instant the flowers popped open.

Every year, without fail, I went to the pond to hear that popping sound. Mutsumi remained the same. She was perpetually distracted, flying off without warning to see her man of the moment, yet keeping me under her spell. I spent twenty years there in her room. Then, one day, I flew into a rage over some trivial matter and strangled her. Just like that, she was gone. Even in death, she seemed distracted. I laid her out on her mattress and walked slowly to the pond in the beech grove. The day was about to break. When it did, a number of lotus flowers opened at the same time. The big blossoms, round and pure white, floated gently on the pond's surface. I invoked the name of Amida Buddha to pacify Mutsumi's soul, and wept.

I REMAINED nameless until the end.

My seventh elder sister, Nanayo, showed up about a year after Mutsumi's death. I had buried Mutsumi beside the pond, and prayed to Amida Buddha for her each day.

Nanayo was most unobtrusive. She built a small hut for herself at the edge of the beech grove, and dwelt within it. I seldom encountered her. The few times I did was when we passed each other in front of the pond. She seemed to be spending long periods of time there. Nanayo's breasts sagged. I guessed that, in former times, they had been firm and full, like the breasts of Ichiko, Mitsue, and Mutsumi. Her hair was turning white, and deep wrinkles were carved around her mouth and eyes.

Nanayo and I rarely spoke to each other. The exceptions were the few times we sat together beside the pond.

"You will die soon," she said to me.

"Soon?" I replied.

"I will die soon too," she went on.

"You too?"

"Your sisters have all died off."

"You mean Futaba and Shima and Goma—they're all dead?"

"Yes, they've all died."

Nanayo's eyes never left the pond as she told me this. Lotus flowers were floating on the water. At some point, they had begun blossoming regardless of the season, in an unending cycle. Whether in summer or winter, spring or fall, there were always at least one or two in full bloom—when plentiful, dozens might be floating on the surface.

Nanayo and I took each other's hand and followed the water trickling from the pond. At first it formed no more than a small stream cutting through the trees, but eventually the flow increased. When it reached the edge of the cliff, it became a waterfall that cascaded down to the world below. Nanayo and I stood at the top and looked. Countless millions of people were milling around down there, in that world. Nanayo spoke. The waterfall is being sucked into its basin, she said. You're right, I replied, it's being sucked in. Still hand in hand, we walked into the waterfall. Then we joined the water and fell. The roar filled my ears. Endlessly, endlessly, we plunged.

Shimazaki

WAS THIS love at first sight? It was my first time, so it threw me for a loop. The man was family from seven generations back, and therefore my—what's the right term? Let's just say an ancestor on my father's side. Anyway, that's who I fell for. You don't have many chances to meet a family member from seven generations back. Running into him was sheer luck. At the time, I had no idea he was my ancestor. Nothing about his features stood out. The only reason he caught my eye was the way his lips twisted slightly when he smiled. It wasn't technically first sight either, for it took me five whole minutes to awaken to the fact that I had fallen in love.

The baby finger on my ancestor's right hand was missing. All the other fingers were skinny and gnarled. His hands bent easily. My ancestor had lost his finger about a hundred and fifty years ago, he said, when he accidentally severed it with a knife.

My ancestor lived alone. He'd been living with a woman, but several years earlier she had walked out. I love women, he said in a quiet voice, but they don't stick around. Where do you live? I asked. Downtown, in a small apartment. He swept back his hair with his four-fingered hand. It's getting too darned long, he muttered. Gets in my eyes. He loathed barbers. Always have, he said. Almost everything else changes with the times, but not barbers—they cling to the old ways, right? My ancestor laughed as he said this. Can I cut it for you? I asked. He opened his eyes wide in surprise. Is it proper to accept such a generous offer from someone I've only just met? Sure it is, I answered. I want to cut it. I really do. I could feel desire seeping into my words. He nodded and, just like that, I was invited to my ancestor's home.

MY ANCESTOR'S apartment house sat halfway down an alley in downtown Tokyo, flanked by a number of identical buildings. It was an old-fashioned sort of apartment house—when he slid open the glass front door, I saw a shoe cupboard in the entryway and, beyond that, a wide hallway with rooms on both sides. The rent here's cheap, he said. My ancestor removed his shoes and placed them in cubbyhole number six. I took off mine and put them in the same cubbyhole. That made it crowded, so I placed his shoes of top of mine, but when he saw that he reversed them, so that my shoes perched on top. Your soles are cleaner than mine. My shoes are heavier too, he said, heading down the hall.

My ancestor's room was on the right side at the end of the hall. I couldn't take my eyes off his fingertips as he inserted the brass key into the lock. I wanted so much to touch them but held back. The wood flooring extended into the apartment to form a small room; beyond that was a tatami room of normal size. The tatami were pretty new. I've just replaced the mats for the first time in ten years, he said. I was a bit down in the dumps after the woman left me. So I asked a tatami maker, a man I've known for ages but whose shop had closed down, to come help me out. He did a great job, like I knew he would. They're cheap, but just having fresh tatami really picks up my spirits. My ancestor placed two teacups on a block that sat on the floor. I can't think of another word than block to describe it. A square, legless box of gleaming black, slightly larger than an apple crate, it could have been solid, in which case it would have weighed a ton, or hollow. A packet of throat lozenges and a tin that had once held dried seaweed were placed on top of it.

My ancestor poured hot water from the kettle into a teapot and from there into our two cups. The rim of one cup was chipped. He took that, and gave me the other. The tea was delicious. That was all it took to elevate my desire for him to new heights. I wanted to move closer, though we were kneeling on the floor. But the room was virtually free of household possessions. A quick scan revealed no fridge, no television, no bookcase, no computer. Not even a telephone. Nothing in the room gave me an excuse to make a move in his direction.

I was listening to the faint sound of him sipping his tea, when he suddenly noticed me staring in his direction. You and I are related by blood, he said. It was only then that I learned my ancestor was indeed my ancestor.

I WANTED us to become real lovers, whatever it took. I had been around a long time, more than two hundred years, but never had I craved anything more. I began to drop by his apartment often. And he always welcomed me, no matter the time of day. He invariably served tea when I arrived. At the beginning, he gave himself the teacup with the chipped rim, but at a certain point he stopped caring who got which cup. The first time he passed me the chipped one, I was so happy I had to grin. What are you smiling about? That's what he said. His voice was soft and gentle. Hearing it turned me on, in the same way that looking at his fingers had. I was just so happy. Because it feels like the barrier dividing us is gone, I answered.

I never noticed that cup was chipped, not once. You've got keen eyes, haven't you, he said with a shrug. But was he really unaware that he had avoided giving me that cup? Or had he consciously refrained from passing it to me at first, and then forgotten all about it? Maybe it had been random, a complete accident. Or, maybe he was simply embarrassed that I had woken to the fact that he had removed what had stood between us. As I was turning all those options over in my head, he poured me another cup of tea.

MY ANCESTOR spent his days in his room. Might he be receiving a pension or something of the sort, I asked? He laughed. Sometimes you sound so formal, he said. No, I get no pension. Pension plans aren't feasible when there are lots of very old folks like me around. It has been determined that I'm able to work, maybe because I still look young. Despite my true age. He blinked a few times as he said this. Later, he explained that, because he was still making money, the pension he might have received had been reduced to "a sparrow's tears"—in other words, to virtually nothing. Since filling out the forms appeared to be a real pain, he had given up on the whole thing.

There was no doubt that my ancestor looked young. He had few white hairs, and his wrinkles weren't all that deep. Most strikingly, his back was still straight. He had long legs. When he strolled down the road, hands in pockets, he looked for all the world like someone whose generation has yet to come on the scene.

My ancestor made his money working as a life coach. His reputation had spread by word of mouth, so that people who had heard of his services sent him letters asking his advice.

The letters had to be certified. If they were express, or registered, or if they came by ordinary mail, he wouldn't answer them. When I asked him why, he said there'd been some trouble in the past. I didn't ask what that trouble was. One thing our many chats had taught me was that my ancestor had no patience with nosy people. If he wanted me to know, he would tell me himself.

His work as a life coach ranged across many topics, from moving house to matchmaking, tracking down lost objects to passing exams. He sent his advice via certified mail as well. That was why he spent most of his days in his room—he was answering all those letters. He would spread out sheets of paper on the block and then compose his answers slowly, using a brush pen.

My mother is a meddlesome woman. What can I do to make her mind her own business? Taito-ku, Tokyo, female (age 73). My wife refuses to have sex with me. I've been begging her every night for ten years, but she hasn't relented once. She is sixty years my junior. I don't want to sleep with other women. How can I get her to soften her attitude? Habikino-shi, Osaka, male (age 230). I have no dreams for the future. I think about killing myself every day. What can I do to find purpose and meaning in life? I need to know. Kushiro-shi, Hokkaido, male (age 16). In exchange for his advice, clients would send him money orders by regular mail. Most were for ten thousand yen, but some were for twenty or thirty thousand; in rare cases, it might amount to more than a hundred thousand yen. My ancestor stuck the money orders in the seaweed tin. When five or so had accumulated, he would go cash them at the post office credit union.

On one of my visits, I found him in the entry putting on

his shoes. Sorry, he said. I'm just on my way to the post office. My ancestor was holding several envelopes in his hand. May I accompany you? I asked. My ancestor laughed. There you go again, acting formal, he said. He strode off, leaving me to hurry after him. Finally, I managed to grab the hem of his jacket. Is it really all right if I come with you? I asked again. Whatever you like, he laughed again. It's just a trip to the post office.

A mere trip to the post office for him, perhaps, but I was thrilled at being able to go along—so thrilled, in fact, that I started to wheeze as I trotted along clinging to his jacket. You may look young, he said, but I can see that you're as old as your age suggests. His voice was gentle. You should take care of yourself. Rest, if you're feeling dizzy. Dizzy or not, I want to be near you, I said. His response was to look up at the sky. It's a beautiful day. How about a bowl of soba? he said, and strode off again. We went to a soba restaurant, where he had chicken and eggs over rice and I had tempura soba.

PEOPLE WHO live to a very old age, like my ancestor and me, aren't what you could call rare these days. One or two hundred years old is commonplace. When I asked my ancestor how old he was, his answer was terribly vague. I can't tell you exactly, he said. Probably a little over four hundred. The thing is, he went on, when you're this old, the days of your youth are so terribly distant. Even your family members—your parents, brothers, and sisters—get lost in the haze. Your personality may have been transformed as well. You can be one kind of person when you're growing up, only to change later. If you meet an old acquaintance again after a hundred years, you're likely to find they've become someone else altogether. Yet they don't look all that different on the surface. That's what's really weird.

I bet you're popular with women, I said. He paused for a long moment. I love women, he said at last. And I've been loved by them as well. But it never lasts that long.

That's exactly what I mean, I said, feeling miffed. Getting involved with one woman after another. And how many children do you have? Grandchildren?

There were three children, I think. Yes, three, I'm sure. I wonder where they are now. There should be a whole pile of grandkids and great-grandkids too. I hope they're all healthy. Health is the key. That and laughter. I love it when you laugh, you know.

Those last words came out of the blue. I was shocked. Seldom had he ever said something sweet like that to me. Because I'm old school, he always said. Old school or new school—it's hard to tell, I thought, when they've been around this long. He poured me another cup of tea. Tea's good for you too, he said. Prevents colds. Come to think of it, I said, my grandmother used to drink buckets of tea. And she lived to a great old age. She's dead now, though. Could she have been one of your descendants, I asked, your child perhaps, or grandchild? No, he said. I don't think so. That's the one who loved diving, right? She was on my father's mother's side. You said so yourself the last time you were here. To tell the truth, the thought that your grandmother could have been one of my descendants did bother me a little.

My ancestor moved his stack of writing paper to one side and set the teacup down. The back of his hand was a little more wrinkled today. I looked at the back of my own hand. It was wrinkled too. I felt a pang of anxiety. What would I do if he died? I had assumed that, having lived so long, he would go on living forever, but there was no guarantee of that. The same went for me. Some of us lived for hundreds of years, while others popped off in their forties or fifties. We wanted to plan ahead, to give our lives some focus, but who knew how long we had? None of us had a glimmer.

HEY, I coaxed, moving closer to him. I climbed up on his lap. Hold me. Please. My ancestor circled his arms around my back. Now we were at the same level. I was a head shorter than he was, so this was the first time we were face to face. I planted my lips on his. He responded a little, but then quickly pulled away. His lips were thin. Thin and hard. Though they had looked soft. Maybe he was rejecting me. Wanting to avoid any hint of incest. It was hard for me to wrap my head around that issue, though. Was our relationship incestuous or not?

I think I'll do some cleaning, my ancestor announced. Then I'll join you, I said. Really? It won't be a burden? If we're doing it together, then I'm happy. My ancestor pulled a duster from the top of the big closet where he stored the bedding. He handed it to me. Then he grabbed a rag and went down the hall toward the shared toilet. My ancestor's room was almost empty, so there weren't many places to dust. All he possessed was a small shelf holding a jumble of plates, books, and clothes, that gleaming black block, and a lamp. A quick rata-tat-tat with the duster and it was all done. I headed down the hall after him.

Hey, I said drawing near, in the same coaxing tone I had

used before. My ancestor had wet the rag and was scrubbing the floor of the toilet. His apartment might have been small, but the shared toilet was pretty big.

I watched him as he wiped the floor, scrubbed the porcelain, and straightened the stack of paper. I'm done dusting, I said. He grunted in acknowledgment. What do you want me to do next? Hearing that, he turned to face me. Don't you know how to clean a room? Certainly. I just thought you might have your own way of doing it.

My ancestor's eyes widened. You're a lot more deferential than I thought, he said. I turned away. I'm not the arrogant bitch you seem to take me for, I replied. Do you really think that's what I'm like? If you got to know me even a little, you'd see that I give people a whole lot of respect. Haven't you figured that out yet? Has all your experience taught you nothing?

This came out in a single burst. My ancestor looked at me with a rapt expression. I've never seen you let it all out like this before. That's the way to do it! Words are there to be used, after all. Whether you're understood or not isn't the point— just let it fly. What have you got to lose?

Words are there to be used? Who was he talking to—the me standing before him or someone else, someone from his past? When it came to talking, I couldn't remember ever holding back. Normally, I was more than able to get out what I wanted to say. My ancestor often mixed up the present with the past like this. There was now and there was back then, there was me and there was another woman from long ago— and suddenly, somehow, things grew confused. When that happened, I would lose my own bearings. Now or then, me or not me? I couldn't tell any more.

Hey, hold me. I sit on my ancestor's lap. There on the chilly wooden floor of the hallway, where someone could come out of their room at any moment, my ancestor holds me on his lap and brings his cheek to mine. I press my cheek against his. His cheek is cold; my cheek is warm. His cheek gradually grows warmer, my cheek gradually grows colder. If only we could be joined together like this forever, I whisper. Yeah, but you're heavy. That's what he said. Heavy, he said again, yet he made no move to push me off. I was turned on. A weird place to get turned on, I thought. Someone came out of their room. On their way to use the toilet, no doubt. My ancestor and I didn't move a muscle. We just froze there, me on his lap, he with his arms around me. A young man slipped by, opened the door to the toilet, then closed it. There was the sound of pissing. A moment later he emerged, shaking water from his hands.

"Hey, Gramps," he said. "You and the old woman had better take care. You'll catch a chill, sitting there like that."

WE STAYED like that, with me on his lap, until the young man closed his door. Gramps, huh, said my ancestor, when he was out of sight. He lowered me to the floor. Don't worry, you're not old. He's just a rude young man. Really.

Returning to my ancestor's room, we swept the floor, scrubbed the shelf and the lamp with a damp cloth, and shut the window, which we had left open. Working like that had mussed my ancestor's hair. I could see a bit of his scalp. Perhaps he had lost all desire for women. That worried me. Glimpsing his scalp just turned me on more. I wrung out the cloth over and over till it was as hard as a rock. My ancestor was sitting beside the block, a vacant expression on his face.

I bet you're tired, he said. You should go home. I could tell my ancestor wanted to be alone. All right, then, I'll see you, I said, and walked out the door. He saw me to the building's entrance. I had been in a situation like this before, I was thinking. But I couldn't pin down when exactly that was. It could have been ten years ago, or fifty, or a hundred and fifty, for that matter—my memory was vague. I had wanted someone, but that someone hadn't wanted me. It had hit me hard. There had been a moment when it felt as if we had joined together as one, but that passed in an instant, leaving uncertainty in its wake. Could I go on living like this? Feeling this alone? I wanted to cradle my head in my hands. Come to think of it, I did have a slight headache. I needed to go home right away and get under the covers. Pour hot water over a spoonful of sweetened kumquats, drink it, and fall asleep. My ancestor was already slipping from my mind. I walked along thinking instead of kumquats. I passed a cat sitting in the middle of the alleyway. It meowed at me. I meowed back.

WHAT SORT of woman was she? I asked my ancestor. I meant the one who had walked out on him a few years earlier. Jealousy can hit you at any age—one never becomes too old for that. I went cross-eyed just imagining him with that woman. And not knowing anything about her was only making those feelings stronger. So I asked him, hoping to bring my emotions under control.

She had very long hair. It was white and twisted into a bun, but at night she would let it down. Sometimes I stepped on it by accident, which hurt her. I suggested that she visit a salon to have it cut short, but she never went. She hated hairdressers as much as I hate barbers, so I couldn't press her too hard. I saw her trimming her own hair once—she pulled it all down over her shoulders and started hacking away. That's a hell of a rough way to do it, I teased, and her nose crinkled with laughter. She was a down-to-earth person.

Why did she walk out?

I don't know. She told me why when she left, but those explanations always fall short. They're like plot summaries of movies and novels—they never manage to touch the heart of the matter.

You think so? I asked.

Yes, I do. The point is, she left me, end of story. My ancestor sounded almost cheerful about this.

I was living with someone until recently too, I said. He hadn't asked, so I volunteered. We lived together for a very long time. About fifty years. But he died. Of old age, I guess.

Old age is hard to categorize these days. Since the human life span isn't set, the only basis for judgment is how far the physical aging process has progressed. No longer is old age determined by how many years someone has lived. A person can be two hundred years old and still die a youthful death. By the same token, an eighty-year-old can die of old age. What is time anyway? I asked my ancestor. It used to be a lot more systematic, back when I was born, he answered. But what about that man? Did you truly love him? You're a fine one to throw "true love" around, I broke in. He looked down at the floor. Here he had come so close to showing jealousy, and I had gone and stopped him.

I can't remember. I've completely forgotten him. Right now, you're the only one I love, I burst out.

Confessing my love only made me sad. My ancestor maintained a certain distance. Like always. Though he never tried to avoid me, we never merged, the way two kinds of liquids blend together. I thought I loved him, but I could never be sure. Maybe I didn't. But, no, that couldn't be. Even now, hearing his voice turned me on. When I looked at his right hand, I longed to take its four remaining fingers in my mouth and suck on them, one by one. In such moments I wanted to have sex. But maybe it wasn't a good idea when I was this sad. It would certainly be better when I was feeling happy. Still, happy or sad, what was the big difference? My ancestor brought his face close to mine and gave me a small kiss. His lips were warm. They were fragrant too, like some kind of flower.

SO MUCH time has passed.

When I stop to count, I realize it's been more than thirty years since my ancestor and I first met. We're still very close. But love at first sight? I remember it happened, but not what it felt like. We still haven't had sex. There were moments when I thought we were going to, but we never did. Perhaps he never really desired me. Yet what's the difference between sex and intimacy? I can find all sorts of ways to define those things in words, yet in the end I don't really know.

My ancestor and I take trips together. He gets fed up with life coaching, he says, and all the letters he has to write. This happens about once every three months. His coaching service has become quite popular. More popular than when we first met. *My father-in-law's debts are dragging us down. He has been using my husband's name to guarantee his loans. Can a son legally disown his father? Chiba City, female (age 32). I live in a village with a dwindling population. Is there any way to convince young people to return here to live? Actually, it's all right if they're not all that young. Okayama-ken, male (age 77). For whatever reason, I have no love for my own children. I have no problem with my grandchildren, my great-grandchildren, even my great-great-grandchildren—it's just my kids I have no affection for. It's been that way since they were little. Will it be like this until I die? Kumamoto City, male (age 157).*

The content of the letters hasn't changed appreciably in thirty years, my ancestor says. It's exhausting—so many people are suffering so much that they're willing to shell out money to get advice. Thank goodness you're here, he mutters.

I know that women are around when I'm not there. This has been going on since he and I got together. Yes, there are women who come to see me, he says as if it's no big deal. It's hard not to respond. But he never responded to me! I worked so hard to make us lovers, yet he has never reciprocated. When I tell him that, he looks me in the eye. Sure, that's what you say. But you don't really love me, do you?

What? I gasped. How can you say that? I've loved you from the beginning. I love you now. So very much.

Are you sure about that? You always act so level-headed. The women who come to see me aren't so cool and composed. They're more devil may care. If I'm going to get close to a woman, that's what I need to feel—that spontaneity. I'm a simple man. I don't think a whole lot. I'm drawn to women in the same way that a plant reaches for the sun, instinctively.

Are you serious? Words escaped me. I was starting to wheeze again.

But I'm glad you're here. You may not love me, perhaps, but I think I do truly love you.

He didn't really mean that a woman had to be spontaneous to be a real woman—I knew that much. He was well aware of the depth of my feelings for him. Nor could I believe that he utterly lacked similar feelings for me. Still, something had kept us from moving forward. A misalignment of some kind. It was sad, and he was trying to cover that sadness with a crude smokescreen of language. He was acting at once sensitive and sly, and it broke my heart.

WE CARRY no luggage on our trips, not even a briefcase. He and I no longer have much in the way of bodily secretions, so we can go several days without changing the clothes we have on. As long as I have my purse, handkerchief, lipstick, and compact I can manage perfectly well.

Our trip reminded us, again, of how many kinds of people there are in the world. Those long-lived like us, though, were far fewer than before. We're dying out, one after another. Seldom did we come across a person of great age, like my ancestor, or even someone as old as me. So much had changed—it felt as if time had just flown by.

Instances of the elderly being knocked down and trampled by the young were common now. My ancestor and I liked to get away to a small island in the northwest, on the Japan Sea. Many of the inhabitants were old. The island was long and narrow. We usually stayed in an inn at its far end. The inn was run by an old couple. A husband and wife, most likely. Though we never asked. I call them an old couple, but they are probably younger than us.

After we arrive at the inn, we take a stroll around the island. We walk clockwise, starting at the tip, in a complete circle. It is early afternoon when we head out, and the sun is already setting when we get back. My ancestor and I sit on the sandy beach and watch the sunset. I hold his hand. One by one, I caress his thumb, his pointer finger, his middle finger, and his ring finger in that order. The skin where his pinky had once been is stretched tight. I miss my ancestor. He is sitting right beside me, but still I miss him as one misses something lost in the distant past. My eyes fill with tears. Hey, hold me. I haven't said those words for a long time. My ancestor puts me on his lap. Heavy, he grunts. Have you gained weight?

I weigh less than I did. But my ancestor has gotten weaker. He could die any day. I cry a little. He does, too. He likely knows his days are numbered. The tip of an island is called Shimazaki—"island point"—he murmurs through his tears. We are crying on Shimazaki, you and I.

It is a beautiful sunset. I remain on his lap for what seems like forever. I kiss his tears away. He kisses mine away too. We blow our noses from time to time. He has tissue paper. I always forget to keep a supply in my pocket, though I do carry a handkerchief. My inability to remember to carry tissues has existed since childhood. I may have forgotten practically everything about my youth, but that I remember.

My ancestor and I cried together for a while. I felt terribly close to him at that moment. Yet in half an hour, when the sunset had faded and darkness had fallen, and we had gone back to the inn to take our bath, the old ambiguity would surely return.

I tested the waters. I truly love you, I said. Do you love

me? My ancestor gave me a faint smile. But he said nothing. I truly love you, I said once more, and threw my arms around him. Would I really feel so sad when he died? I thought maybe not. Then again, I might go out of my mind. Either way, my own death wouldn't be nearly so sad.

I love you. I murmured it over and over again. There on my ancestor's lap, looking out at the setting sun of Shimazaki.

Sea Horse

IT HAS been ages since I left the sea.

Now I live in Tokyo, on the fringes of Setagaya. Two run-down video rental stores sit side by side in front of the station, and beside them an old tofu store and a pastry shop selling cakes and, as of five years ago, fresh-baked bread. Across the tracks, a supermarket. Its doors stay open until 10 pm. A local market used to be there, but it was torn down some years ago and the supermarket built in its place.

My husband is a transport company executive. His office is in downtown Tokyo. The company's headquarters are in Hiroshima. He always comes home late.

How long has it been since I was handed over to my current husband? Thirty years? I can't remember exactly.

We have four children.

The oldest boy has a job in Aichi, doing computer-related work. The next two are twins: one lives in a university dormitory in northeastern Japan while the other works at part-time jobs, crashing at his friends' homes or, sometimes, here. The fourth child, our only daughter, dropped out of high school and now works nights in one of those video stores (the one closer to the tracks).

The fourth child can't wake up in the morning. I took her to the hospital for a checkup, but all I got from the doctor was that she was suffering from orthostatic something or other. Is that the name of a disease, I asked? No, he said. My daughter and I trudged home carrying a mountain of vitamins and blood-strengthening medicines. Neither of us said a word.

This husband comes home late. The one before worked at home. He was a painter. I modeled for him any number of times. He saw something wild and untamed in my body, so he always made me pose naked. "Clothes don't suit you," he would say. "You put them to shame." As I recall, one of his portraits of me won some sort of prize. No one talks about him anymore, though. He is totally forgotten. He had been feeding me for about twenty years when he announced he had tired of me and handed me over to my current husband.

Apparently, the artist passed away not long after that. I can't read very well, and TV exhausts me, so I never learned exactly when or how. It was more than ten years later when, quite out of the blue, my current husband let it drop that the artist had died a long time ago. "Is that so?" I asked. "Yes," he answered. And that was that.

The husband before the artist was a university professor, and the one prior to that was a rich merchant who owned a lot of land. I have only a vague recollection of my husbands before the war. I think a tycoon of some sort and a viscount from some place or other are mixed in there somewhere, but I can't be certain.

So many husbands, yet until I was handed over to this one, only one child. It was born when I was with the merchant landowner, but it lived less than three years. I suppose half-human children don't have the staying power that others do. In fact, I regarded its survival to that point as a kind of miracle.

That baby's grave is there even now, in the cemetery at

Zoshigaya. I go there occasionally to offer incense. After my daughter dropped out of school, she and I began visiting the grave from time to time during our outings. On the way back, we would stop by a dessert cafe in Ikebukuro, where she would order *shiruko* sweet red bean soup and I the *mitsumame* gelatin cubes in syrup. Then we would catch the Yamanote Line to Shinjuku and transfer to the private railroad that took us home.

TEMPTATION LURED me from the sea.

It was night. The air was warm and carried the fullness of spring. I had raised myself half out the water to breathe it all in when another, more powerful aroma wafted from the shore.

I have but a dim image of my other husbands, but my memory of the first is as clear as day.

The man had a strong odor. He was brimming with an inner fierceness. I could search the oceans, I thought, and never find another man like this one. That inner force circulated throughout his body, heating his blood. His physical presence was overpowering.

I swam to shore, leapt up on land and made a beeline for him. I couldn't hold back, not even for a second.

I rushed up to him. He looked a little surprised, but his hesitation quickly vanished.

We spent the next few months together. His home was a rough shack on the water. The winds sometimes blew the roof away, and when the waves were high the floor was swamped.

He was a fisherman, but he was better suited to trolling for women than trolling for fish. Even after my arrival he continued playing around. Sometimes he would bring a woman back to the shack. I would sit there in the dark and watch intently as they copulated.

When they had finished, the man would always chase the woman away. Not that any of them needed much encouragement. The man's reputation in the village was far from savory. As soon as the woman left, the man and I would waste no time setting to it ourselves. Warm breezes blew through the walls as the lapping tides slowly soaked the shack.

After six months of this, I was passed on to the boss of the village, the man the fishermen relied on. My own man was flat broke.

This new man gave off the fragrance of incense. His skin was very fair. I immediately tried to return to the sea, but to no avail. He placed a metal ring around my neck and linked it to a long chain bolted to a stake. I could move only as far as the chain allowed, which meant I couldn't leave the room.

The furnishings of the room were luxurious, the bedding always sheathed in fine silk. In the corner was a painted screen decorated with images of beautiful kimono, and tucked behind it a fancy ceramic chamber pot for me to use.

I was angry, though, and refused to squat over that thing. But every time I made a mess, my husband thrashed me. I howled bloody murder each time that happened. He may have smelled strangely sweet, and his skin may have been fair, but he was still awfully strong.

For years, I lived chained up like that. When I shed tears of longing for the sea, the waves rose in response. Violent storms increased, and young people moved away, so the village fell on hard times.

The fishermen's boss passed me on to my next husband. He lived in the mountains, far from the sea.

MY CURRENT husband says our fourth child is my spitting image.

She's a strapping young woman, that's for sure. Once, back when she was still in high school, she brought her classmates over to visit. They were all compactly built with skin darkened by the sun. They talked and laughed incessantly.

My daughter sat among them, quiet as a mouse. She seemed at a loss what to do with her body, so big and soft and white among all her tanned friends.

My first three children are all boys. Two resemble my husband, the other doesn't. Not one of them looks like me. Only my daughter does.

The days when I would rail against my husbands, weeping and mourning my loss of the sea, ended decades ago. I came to feel almost completely human, especially after my children were born. It reached the point that, most of the time, I myself forgot that I was different.

Although my first child was sickly and died before the age of three, my four children with my current husband haven't been sick a day in their life. They may be half-human, but they developed very much like human children. In body and in character too, they leave a distinctly human impression.

There were signs, though, that the fourth child would turn out differently. She somehow stood out from the human crowd. It wasn't that noticeable when she was young, but as she got older it became more evident. By the time she started high school I could see how much her spirit diverged from that of the other students. It wasn't just that she was bigger; there was also something vast and boundless about her. While years and years of training had tamed my spirit, hers was like mine once had been. Looking at her, I felt as though my original self had been reborn.

It seems that my daughter was picking up boys at her job in the video rental shop. Or maybe she was the one being picked up. She would go to their rooms, but according to her they never had sex or even fooled around. Really? I asked. Then what do you do?

We just hang out, she replied. Playing games, watching videos, sending emails.

You play games?

Yeah, one of us plays while the other talks on the cellphone.

My fourth child told me all this in snatches, with stretches of silence sandwiched in between. She doesn't volunteer much, but she'll answer when I ask. Her father finds it hard to deal with her, so he's stopped trying. He comes home later and later now that the three boys aren't around so much.

Why don't you have sex? I asked her.

Because I don't feel like it.

Have you ever done it?

No.

You could give it a try.

I will eventually.

My fourth child almost never misses work at the video shop. Even on her off days, she's always willing to fill in for her colleagues if asked. The shop at night relaxes her, she says. It feels like the night sea.

I sometimes think back on the sea at night. It has been an eternity since I left.

MOST OF my husbands treated me well.

They kept me well fed and clean in fine rooms, and decked me out in nice clothes. I was always at their beck and call, like a well-maintained car in their garage.

I wanted to return to the sea as soon as possible. That awful ring around my neck was eventually removed, yet the sea grew more and more distant as I was passed from husband to husband. To reach the coast, I would have had to change trains, and I didn't know how. I tried to escape a number of times but always failed. They quickly caught me and brought me back. Then they thrashed me. Once I had been cleaned up and beautifully clothed again, they abused me however they pleased.

As long as I didn't try to escape, each of them was kind to me. Yet behind that kindness was an absence of any real concern, as if they were dealing with a small animal. A chilliness.

Was it something in me—that part of me that humans lacked, perhaps—that made my husbands behave in such a way? After climbing up on land, I tried so hard for so many years to fit in with my husbands, with people in general. Yet, in the end, I failed.

I came to accept my lot. As long as they treated me well, I was satisfied. My memories of the sea grew ever fainter. It was so remote. I hadn't laid my eyes on it in such a long time. It felt like forever.

There seems to be a verbal agreement that passes between my husbands each time I am handed from one to the next. This is the injunction: "Never let her near the ocean."

Yes, this has been their motto. She who comes from the sea must be kept from the sea. Otherwise, she will return.

All my husbands have followed this dictum. Now I am living in the Setagaya neighborhood in Tokyo. I could reach the ocean, I suppose, if I changed trains several times. But I have already forgotten what it's like. And trying to remember that which one has forgotten is terribly painful. It's like searching for the eye of a tiny needle at the bottom of a deep hole, only worse.

I am not human. Yet now I live completely surrounded by human beings. Having children made it that way. I no longer weep for my beloved ocean. My current husband seems not to be taking the injunction too seriously. Our children have been to the sea on several occasions. My husband is the one who took them. I always stayed at home, the excuse being that I was under the weather. The first three children embraced the sea. Only the fourth refused to go near the water. According to my husband, she wouldn't budge an inch, stiffening her body and wailing, her face crimson.

That fourth child has a name. I told her what it was on the occasion of her first period. It is not to be rashly spoken aloud. It can be used only when absolutely necessary.

My first child has no name. Neither does the second or the third. They have human names of course, but not real names. Only the fourth child's name came to me. It threaded its way through the night sea and the chilly air to where I lay. I had just given birth.

My legs were still spread when they took the baby and placed it on my chest to be nursed. It took to the breast with great enthusiasm, though it had just come into the world.

At first the milk just oozed, but the baby sucked so hard that before long it was gushing out. Thick, rich milk dribbled from the corners of the baby's mouth. One by one, the drops landed on my skin.

I have a real name too. None of my husbands has heard it. Not even the first. I have spoken it aloud only rarely, even back when I was living in the ocean, and to do that I had to swim to the northernmost reaches where no one lives and whisper it behind the rocks on the seabed.

Drawn to my voice, the shrimp and starfish left their hiding places and swam to me. Transparent jellyfish leisurely wove their way through my long, trailing hair. Although I was living in the ocean, I had never really taken to it. I didn't mix much with those like me, but chose to roam the northern waters alone. I told no one my name, and no one told me theirs. On and on I swam through the frigid sea, silently mingling with its creatures.

My fourth child stands behind the counter of the video rental store, so large and pale and out of place. I sometimes walk down to the station at night just to get a glimpse of her. I don't go inside, but stand a bit away in a spot that affords a view of the bright interior. A woman coming home from work passes through the station wicket and is sucked into the store. A young man on a bicycle emerges from the dark streets and is sucked in as well. My fourth child barely notices them passing before the counter, as if gazing out at an endless landscape.

I quietly call her name as I watch her from the darkness. Bathed in the fluorescent lights, she has no idea I am there. Their brightness makes her form blurry, indistinct. There in the cold light, she seems to be melting away.

After a while I head home. My husband isn't back yet. He seldom catches even the last train these days. Sometimes I am awakened by the closing of a taxi door, but by three in the morning, the hour of the Ox, I am fast asleep. A few hours later, my fourth child comes home after her shift. Our house is used to these late-night comings and goings. Small night creatures squeeze in through the tiny holes in the wall. The trapped air of day seeps into the great outdoors through the cracks in the windows. In my bed, I sense past husbands riding the night air to reach me. They spin about me in circles, gather on the ceiling. When morning comes, they will go back to where they came from. In my dreams, I try to picture their faces. But they are all so vague. Like the firefly squid of the northern sea, they flash on and off, off and on, always eluding my grasp.

My own name is half-forgotten. It has been so very long since I tried to remember it.

I HAVE been close to the sea only once in all these years.

My husband at the time was a strange man. He was seldom home. Instead, he lived on the road, seeking out the heart of the mountains and the ends of the sea. Whatever he brought back he crammed into his house, his private citadel. Marble busts of women and men. Fabrics of all colors. Roots of trees. Stuffed animals, examples of the taxidermist's art. Rattan baskets with lids. Old leather-bound books. Atlases.

He was not at home when I was passed on to him. One month elapsed, then two, and still he had not appeared. I staved off starvation by drinking quantities of tap water. When there is no food, I am quite able to subsist on water alone.

Then one day the taps went dry. Apparently, my husband

hadn't paid his water bill. There was a river nearby, so I went out to soak in it. We were in a city, though, so it was encased in concrete and had wire fencing strung along its banks. I had to wait until night, when no one was around. I climbed over the fence, shed my clothes, and hopped in. The river was shallow. Water weeds longer than my hair twined about my arms and legs. Large carp poked my sides as I drank. The water tasted awful.

The river grew wider and deeper as I floated downstream. I passed schools of carp, big and small. They stayed in a single place, while I was moving.

How long did I drift before I realized I was nearing the ocean? Several days, perhaps. When I smelled it on the air I began to grow worried. No, a voice inside me was whispering. You shouldn't return to the ocean yet. It was autumn. Rows of soft clouds ranged high above me, a mackerel sky. As I floated along on my back, I thought no, the time has not yet come. The ocean was tempting me, though. Just as my first husband had. My body was being pulled in its direction. But my heart stood opposed. This clash continued for some time.

Finally, I reversed course and began to swim upstream. Slowly at first, then more rapidly. Schools of small fish made way for me as my streamlined form cut through the water. It had been so long since I swam like that. My whole body rejoiced, from my fingertips to my flanks, my crotch to my toes. Now I was flying through the water, my hair streaming behind.

It was late at night when I arrived at my husband's home. I was lying there, my wet hair spread out on the floor, when he came back.

"Welcome home," I said.

"Is it you?" he said. "Can it really be you?" He dropped his big backpack on the floor and began fondling my body, exploring every part with his hands. I had just emerged from the water, so I was stark naked.

"You were trying to go back to the ocean, weren't you," he said. His fondling grew rougher. I knew his behavior was outrageous, but I let him do what he wanted. After all, I had been handed over to him.

He kept at me throughout the night, abusing my body as he pleased. I didn't feel anything. None of the elation I had experienced with my first husband remained, not a speck. When light returned to the sky and the red, overripe sun began to ooze over the horizon, he finally released me.

From then until he departed on his next trip, my husband rarely used me, and then only as if he had suddenly recalled my presence. Instead, I was left to lie unwanted like all the other objects he had collected on his travels.

I slept quietly among his sculptures. Those of women usually portrayed the upper half, those of men the lower.

When I opened my eyes, he was often seated at a desk in the middle of the room, eating or smoking a cigarette, or jotting something down on manuscript paper. All I could see from where I lay was his back. It was thick and struck me as somehow desolate.

The night before he left on his next trip, he handed me over to my next husband. First, he stripped me naked and jammed me into a crate. Then, heedless of its weight, he hoisted the crate on his shoulder and carried me all the way to my new home. My body was twisted every which way, my limbs at all angles—I could barely breathe as I bounced along.

When we arrived at my new husband's home, my old husband threw the crate down on the floor of the entranceway. My hair popped out one end, my feet out the other. My new husband cried out in surprise. I had smelled the sea while in the crate. The odor came from my own body.

I crawled from the crate. I looked up at my former husband's face. It showed no emotion whatsoever. My new husband thanked him, and he left. I kept my eye fixed on that thick, somehow desolate back as it disappeared down the road.

"A STORM is coming," my fourth child says.

"Even though it's winter?" I ask.

"It's a really big one," she says, shaking her head. "We've got to escape."

"Escape to where?"

"To the ocean."

Startled, I look at her face. Flames are shooting from its center. There should be no flames, yet there they are. Her face is shining. At that moment I realize she is about to leave for good. The other three had left, but they still came back from time to time. This one wouldn't. I would never see her again.

"What will you do when you reach the ocean?" I ask.

"I don't know. But I'm half from the ocean anyway. Originally."

"There's nothing there," I say.

"There's nothing here on land either."

"There are men, aren't there?"

"Yeah, such as they are."

Such as they are. For many long years men have looked

after me, passed me around, made me do their bidding. I want to tell all that to my daughter, but I doubt she will understand. Then why didn't you leave earlier? she'll ask. The fact you didn't leave means that you really didn't want to. What could I possibly say in my defense?

I tried to remember my first man. But I couldn't. Why have I spent so long so far from the sea? I thought of the husband with the desolate back who had jammed me into a crate and carried me off. Was he still scouring the ends of the earth in his search? Or had he died long ago?

That husband had lavished my body with endless caresses before he packed me in the crate. Each of my husbands seemed to have grown sad as time passed, regarding me with eyes of unquenchable longing. Once he had climaxed inside me, though, this one briskly crammed me in a box, deaf to my groans. I'll show you what real suffering is, he muttered as he jammed me further in.

Were any of them from the sea? Did any have true names?

A storm is on the way. Every night my fourth child says this.

WHEN THE storm finally hits, it blacks out our whole neighborhood. Both video shops in front of the station close their shutters. The supermarket closes before its usual 10 pm too. I grab my umbrella and walk to pick up my fourth child at her workplace to take her home. The wind is strong—it's all I can do to hang on to the umbrella. The awning of the video shop is flapping madly. Eyes sparkling, my child is standing beneath the wet and darkened awning. She is drenched too.

I stop and look at her from a slight distance. Water is

streaming from her large white body. She is laughing happily. As the rain pelts her, I can hear her peals of laughter.

"Are you leaving?" I ask her.

"You bet," she answers with a laugh.

"Don't go."

"I'm going."

"But there's nothing good about the ocean."

"You needn't worry about me."

Still laughing, she runs out into the rain. I stand and watch her, still from a distance. My child is leaving me. My eyes take in nothing but her. Her back is growing smaller. The way she runs is strange—she seems to be dancing, yet there is something uncertain in her stride. When she reaches the river beyond the tracks she leaps in headfirst, not bothering to remove her clothes. The river is a torrent in the storm.

I see her head sink beneath the surface, then rise again. She is drifting away with the current, but I am rooted to the spot. I try calling her back, but my voice is lost in the wind. I can't even hear it myself.

Soon she is out of sight. I call her by her true name. I can feel a trace of her return. It timidly joins me under my umbrella. For a second, her warmth envelops me. Then she is gone. I weep.

The blackout lasts all night. My husband doesn't come home. I lie on our bed thinking of the fish that live in the sand at the bottom of the ocean, their almost imperceptible movements.

"I WANT to go to the sea."

"The sea?" my husband says.

"Take me there," I ask him.

"What will you do there?"

"Return. I want to return."

"So, the time has come, then."

My husband puts me in the car, and we set off for the sea. A gale is blowing. It has been blowing nonstop since the night my fourth child left. We drive from Setagaya to Tamagawa Avenue, then get on the Metropolitan Expressway. The wind pounds the side of the car, making it shake. When we reach the Tomei Highway the traffic suddenly gets heavier.

At Atsugi, we exit the expressway and take a road through the mountains to Oiso.

"You seem to know the way," I say to my husband. He nods.

"I come here sometimes," he says.

"Why?"

"To look at the ocean," he says. Sadness is written on his face. He too is yearning for something.

The wind is getting stronger and stronger. Not a soul can be seen on the beach at Oiso. The fishing boats are moored out on the water. The sky is leaden. A dull light stretches out from the horizon.

"Are you all right with me going back?" I ask my husband.

"That which comes from the ocean must return to the ocean," he answers. "Keeping you here has been exhausting for all of us," he continues. "Go ahead—I won't try to stop you."

Hearing those words makes me weak in the knees. I have forgotten the sea for so long. Indeed, I am hard put to recall my true name.

The trees on the other side of the road are whipping back

and forth in the wind. The sign for a fishermen's lodge comes crashing to the ground. I put my foot in the water, my body shaking. The image of my fourth child's form melting under the video shop's fluorescent lights comes back to me with perfect clarity. I can feel the water soaking my shoes. Where in the ocean would my child be by now?

Quietly, I step out further. A few steps away from shore. Now the water reaches my thighs.

I can hear the shoreline murmuring loudly. All sorts of things are being blown about in the wind. Hundreds of winged insects are plastered to my body.

Now the water is up to my neck. Is my husband still watching me from the beach?

I look back, but the waves block my view. My clothes have melted away at some point, and a jet-black pelt is beginning to cover my body. The smell of the sea envelops me. I can feel my forelegs and my hindlegs sprouting muscles and my torso thickening. My neck is growing longer; a thick mane sprouts from my head.

I am a sea horse once again, swimming the seas. I pass the moored fishing boats and race toward the horizon, gaining momentum as I go. Days and nights pass as I speed along. When I reach the northern reaches of the ocean, I can picture my fourth child swimming ahead. Her laughter rings in my ears. On and on I run. To that point in the ocean where day and night come to an end.

ABOUT THE AUTHOR AND TRANSLATOR

HIROMI KAWAKAMI is one of Japan's most popular novelists. Many of her books have been published in English, including *Manazuru*, *The Nakano Thrift Shop*, *Parade*, *Record of a Night Too Brief*, *Strange Weather in Tokyo* (shortlisted for the Man Asian Literary Prize in 2013), and *The Ten Loves of Nishino*. *People from My Neighborhood*, translated by Ted Goossen, was published in 2020.

TED GOOSSEN is the editor of *The Oxford Book of Japanese Short Stories*. He translated Haruki Murakami's *Wind/Pinball* and *The Strange Library*, and co-translated (with Philip Gabriel) *Men Without Women* and *Killing Commendatore*.